THE HAND

PART II

A Young Man Discovers What Lies Beyond Eternity's Gate

Lynn Van Praagh-Gratton
with
Brett Stephan Bass

First published by Dog Ear Publishing
4011 Vincennes Rd
Indianapolis, IN 46268
www.dogearpublishing.net

ISBN: 978-1-4575-5791-0

This book is printed on acid-free paper.

This book is a work of fiction. References to real people, events, establishments, organizations, or locales are intended only to provide a sense of authenticity, and are used fictitiously. All characters, and all incidents and dialogue, are drawn from the authors' imagination and are not to be construed as real.

Printed in the United States of America

ALSO BY BRETT STEPHAN BASS:

DESTINY'S ASSASSIN

EULOGY

PURSUIT

THE BENCH

THE HAND (Part 1)...
   A Young Man's Search for Eternity's Gate

THE JOURNEY

THE LETTER

THE RIVALRY

REDEMPTION

WIND CHIMES

WHY?

"There are more things in heaven and earth, Horatio, Than are dreamt of in your philosophy."

William Shakespeare, *"Hamlet"...Act 1, scene 5*

"The day which we fear as our last is but the birthday of eternity."

Lucius Annaeus Seneca (4 BCE – 65 CE)

The challenge of life
is to overcome adversity
and to make good use of the days
we are privileged to live.

This work, a collaboration, is written with the fullness of our hearts, and is dedicated to... you, our reader, to offer...
Understanding
Healing
Hope

INTRODUCTION

Fate is as unpredictable as a sudden summer storm sending cascading waters from a cloud-consumed sky intent on cleansing the earth. How Lynn and Brett were brought together in 2015 leaves chance behind and probes for a deeper meaning lying in a destination that the two have come to call *Beyond the Beyond*. Why were they brought together? To collaborate to try to lift the veil of "cosmic existence" in order to make sense of mankind's place in the universe; a task which is both challenging and rewarding.

Each partner in this project has been entrusted with a precious and unique gift. *Lynn Van Praagh-Gratton*, since childhood, was endowed with the ability to hear the words and feel the feelings of those who have surrendered their flesh to mother earth and who now carry on in a newborn reality. Lynn has traveled around the country addressing large groups and serving individual clients with healing messages received from lost loved ones who want to comfort those left behind. Her remarkable talent has earned her a reputation as a "spiritual healer."

Brett Stephan Bass, on the other hand, at age 62, awoke one morning welcoming an unexpected guest to his life who delivered something remarkable and, at the same time, bewildering...the gift of auto-writing. And, for the next seven years, Brett self-published eleven novels that blended science, philosophy, history, and religion to fashion "life narratives." Each story arrived fully written in his mind with a title attached; one followed by another and yet another and still another. In weeks, not months, he sketched stories on paper that resonated with the heart and traveled to the soul. Never once did he experience writer's block. Never once did he need to rewrite paragraphs. Never once did his pen stumble as it wove an elegant tapestry of cathartic emotions. How could this be? Destiny? If so, a destiny authored by who or what and for what reason?

It was a chance meeting that brought a psychic-medium and an author together in 2015. Or was it chance or perhaps...a *hand*, a "*spiritual hand?*"

In his eleventh novel, "The Hand...A Young Man's Search for Eternity's Gate," Brett introduced his reader to Emerson Alexander Weiss, a wunderkind. Described by his professors at Stanford University as "a blossoming Einstein," Emerson suspends thoughts of becoming a theoretical physicist, blown by the winds of change off course by a chain of events that challenged his understanding of existence and perceived reality. Forsaking science, philosophy, and religion, he embarked upon a journey to discover what seemed unreachable...*Eternity's Gate*. Remarkably, he does find its entry!

Once you follow Emerson's footsteps in Part I of his sojourn, you will yearn to know more. Much more about... life, death, rebirth, and the transmigration of human consciousness to a domain of "pure light and love." And, in Part II, Lynn will call upon her years of mentoring and healing to reveal "what lies beyond *Eternity's Gate*" in this continuing account of Emerson's journey.

When both books are paired together, like the pairing of a psychic-medium and an author, it is hoped that the message that cleaves to your heart is:

"The day which we fear as our last is but the birthday of eternity."

FIFTY*

E merson was drawn by the light escorted on a majestic carpet of illu-
mination to a destination that was *Beyond the Beyond*. It happened in
immeasurable time, no longer than the blink of a cosmic eye reduced in
duration ten thousand fold. His flesh had been left behind as unnecessary
baggage, freely abandoned and forgotten, a mere vestige of discarded
waste like a chrysalis forsaken by a newly released butterfly which was
eager to soar unrestrained from its imposed confinement. His memories
were preserved in full chronicling four disparate lifetime experiences with
the promise that no more would be added. Why? Because no more were
needed to complete the circle of earthly belonging. The eternal universe
had finally welcomed him home and, to greet him, it embraced him with
the purest distillation of perfected love. And, he felt at peace much like a
newborn in the protective embrace of a first time mother.

Their anguish was indescribable and seemingly emotionally insur-
mountable. "How could it be?" Milka and Josip challenged all reason. As a
father's quivering hand hastily summoned the police, eventually pleading
in a fractured tone for assistance, his heart told him what his mind already
knew. That their son, Emerson Alexander, no longer breathed life at an age
that had extended only halfway between 18 and 19.

The cause of death reported on the coroner's death certificate was
eventually divorced of an explanation, reading in bold italicized print
"UNKNOWN," insensitive and uncaring when read over and over and

---

Authors' Note: This chapter heading begins at FIFTY continuing, with continuity, the
story of "The Hand...A Young Man's Search for Eternity's Gate" written by Brett
Stephan Bass.

over again by a mother with a heart aching for answers. All that remained to provide consolation was a note left by Emerson that clung to his pillow as he lay lifeless on the floor which concluded with these words:

'The day which we fear as our last is but the birthday of eternity.'
Please, don't mourn my passing. Rather, celebrate that I have
finally found eternal life and eventually you will as well!

With A Love That Can Never Die,
Emerson

Cryptic words of consolation had been penned to deliver hope but were deprived of digestible meaning to assuage parental grieving. Searing shock waves of anguish coursed through the neural pathways of two brains begging for anesthetizing relief. But all that arrived was a never ending ocean of salt-laden tears!

Emerson Alexander Weiss would have protested, had he had a voice, that he did not want a traditional Jewish burial given the fact that he had refused to have a *bar mitzvah,* shattering his parents' hopes in a fit of defiance in June 1958, twenty-one months before his thirteenth birthday. Dispensing with what he called "mythology born of ignorance," Emerson judged his religion, and all others as well, to be what Einstein had called four years earlier: "The expression of human weakness." As for Milka and Josip Weiss, Judaism was more than an article of faith. It was a way to connect to the past and to cling to hope in the future. Therefore, they followed the traditions established by their forefathers in planning for their son's funeral which would take place on Sunday, September 19, 1965.

In preparing Emerson's remains for burial, three steps needed to be attentively followed: washing (*rechitzah*), purification (*taharah*), and dressing (*halbashah*). A simple wooden casket was chosen free of adornment. There was no lining and no hint of embellishment. Since Emerson never wore a prayer shawl, a winding sheet was substituted and was laid into the casket to receive Emerson's lifeless body. Now wrapped, Rabbi Ephraim Oshry, who had succeeded Benjamin Fleischer at the Beth Hamedrash Hagodol Synagogue, sprinkled soil (*afar*) from Eretz Israel over various parts of Emerson's body and the interior of the casket. Then, the cover was closed and prepared for transfer to Mount Lebanon Cemetery in Glendale, Queens, New York.

A light misty rain began to fall as Milka, Josip, and friends followed Rabbi Oshry and the casket in a procession to the gravesite that had already been prepared to receive a once vibrant young man who believed that he would become a Nobel Prize winning theoretical physicist; but fate had other plans for him. Dispensing with a service conducted at a funeral home, Milka and Josip requested an abbreviated service at the cemetery to abridge a tearful farewell.

The funeral ceremony was brief. The rabbi recited psalms from a prayer book that was tattered from age and repetitive usage. Delivering a eulogy which was laced with powerful emotions that vibrated like the strings of a harp intending to bring soothing solace, God's servant on earth finished with a traditional Jewish prayer called *El Moley Rachamim*. All that remained was to return soil to its original resting place. And so, following another Jewish tradition, mourners took turns throwing three shovelfuls of dirt into the grave with the point of the tool pointing down instead of up "to show the antithesis of death to life."

Upon returning home, Milka and Josip were comforted by those attending the funeral who were inspired to share memories of Emerson and to express the hope that God would attenuate their loss by nourishing their hearts with love. Again honoring tradition, Milka and Josip refrained for a week from bathing, and a distraught father allowed his beard to grow untouched. They did not wear leather shoes or jewelry. They covered all mirrors to shield their reflections. And they sat for hours on low stools which, in their religion, was symbolic of being "brought low" by the onset of grief and mourning. During this period of time called *shiva*, Hebrew for "seven," Josip and Milka received a never vanishing flow of visitors who provided compassion and kindness in an act called a *mitzvah*, bringing food and comforting caring.

Seven days of retreating from daily routines evaporated and slowly did the tears that seemed immune from mercy. Necessity insisted that Josip return to his haberdashery shop and Milka to her duties as a homemaker. Mirrors were restored to their original purpose and low stools were bequeathed to a Jewish charity. An apartment that once held three was now despondently reduced to two. And a bedroom that once welcomed a son had its door securely closed to hold back a reminder of what was and what was hoped to be.

FIFTY-ONE

Milka Weiss was consumed by determined despair that gnawed at her heart like a child taking small bites from an apple intent on leaving nothing more than a useless core. As she wandered aimlessly to a destination left to chance, the temperatures were retreating as September surrendered to October and the leaves, now bursting with color, were preparing to wither away and litter the landscape. It was a bitter reminder of nature's rhythmical cycle of life and death followed by renewal. Upon reflection, the imagery invited Milka to recall Emerson's three reincarnation experiences that led him on a quest to find the meaning of life that resided beyond Eternity's Gate.

It was a bench perfected by an arm's length view of the flowing Hudson River that offered solace to tired legs and a troubled psyche. And Milka welcomed a moment of tranquility to collect and catalogue her thoughts.

Then a memory returned from the distant past. She and Josip were lying on a blanket by the Drava River in their hometown of Osijek, Croatia. It was mid-July 1940, a year before they were forced to flee to avoid arrest and deportation to a death camp meant for Jews and other minorities during a tumultuous time of conquest and sadistic hatred. Milka recalled being bathed by the warmth of the Sun discarding cares and embracing love's vitality—two hearts with synchronizing heartbeats. Suddenly, a movie replayed that moment in time in her head and the words stored away for twenty-five years returned as though they had been spoken just minutes ago:

"You know what I love about you, Milka?"
"What Josip?"
"Everything!"
"Everything?"
"Yes Milka, everything! It's just that you make me so happy to be alive. When I wake up in the morning, my first thought is to reach out to feel for you to make sure that my life is real, not a falsified dream. I can't

imagine, not for a single moment, not breathing the air you breathe. If God took you away from me, I swear upon His name that I would throw myself, feet first, into the Drava River and settle upon the bottom never to rise to the top."

As quickly as the narrative arrived, it departed from Milka's waking memory. And, almost involuntarily, she rose from the bench and walked a short distance to a grassy area that hugged the Hudson River and welcomed a fisherman's line or venturing wading feet.

"Throw myself, feet first, into the Hudson River," crept into Milka's despondent mind, substituting one river for another. "To join Emerson in a place that lies beyond Eternity's Gate," she encouraged herself in a moment of deluded confusion.

One step forward, however, led quickly to two steps back propelled by the intervention of an involuntary force. Unbeknownst to a grieving mother suffering from a fractured heart, fate had arrived to avert a tragic ending to what had been an earlier tragic ending weeks before. Why? Why did Milka retreat from temptation? Because providence was about to introduce her to a remarkable woman who was endowed with a gift, a gift that would allow a mother to converse with a departed son!

"I'll have none of it!" bellowed Josip at the height of his lung capacity. "It's the work of the Devil. It's playing with fire! It violates God's commandments! It's a cruel trick to manipulate your emotions while your wallet is being picked clean."

"But she comes highly recommended," was Milka's urgent retort.

"Recommended?" laughed Josip. "Your good friend Sarah Tishman had a great recommendation to cure my persistent constipation. Remember?"

"Yes dear."

"She swore that it was a miracle cure. 'Dip 10 to 12 dry grapes without seeds into milk and then boil the milk,' she preached. 'Then drink the milk separately and then chew the grapes.' And...."

"You got nauseous, dear."

"And?"

"Well, you know Josip."

"Stuff came out of my mouth. Not my ass!"

"Ok. But this is different."

"How so?"

"Remember when I had thoughts of throwing myself into the Hudson River to end my pain?"

"Yes Milka. I told you to meet with Rabbi Oshry for grief counseling."

"Well, as we both know, his words were kind but not very helpful."

"So, my next suggestion was that you meet with Dr. Millstone, the psychiatrist who had hypnotized Emerson and brought our son back in time when he lived three separate past lives in Argentina, Jordan, and Peru."

"Yes Josip. And now the good doctor has taken no money from me and has offered consoling words."

"Words that remind me of the saying…'You get what you pay for.'"

"Josip, Dr. Millstone gave me the name of a powerful healer who he called a psychic-medium. He said that he had several readings with her. 'Skeptical at first,' were his exact words, he tried to challenge the integrity of her reputation."

"And?"

"He failed! Dr. Millstone said that the healer brought him to a place where departed souls reside. And…and…."

"And what, Milka? What came to his eyes and ears? Words from the grave? Spirits appearing out of thin air? An accurate weather prediction? The winner of this year's baseball World Series between Los Angeles and Minnesota?"

"You can joke all you like, Josip; but, Dr. Millstone, as you know, is well-respected in his field and was a powerful influence on Emerson's understanding of his life."

"Well then, the good doctor, who I do respect, said what?"

"The woman in question connected him to his dead father, maternal grandmother, and a beloved aunt, each sending messages meant only for his ears and no other."

"What is this fortune-teller's name?"

"She's no fortune-teller. Her brain is somehow able to channel words from the land of the dead to that of the living. Quite a difference from predicting that you're going to come into money or you are going to take a trip."

"Ok. If Dr. Millstone vouches for her, then there is little to lose except *hope* if she turns out to be a fraud. Her name is?"

"Lynn Van Praagh-Gratton."

"How do we get in touch with this Van person?"

"Van Praagh-Gratton, dear."

"OK, how do we get in touch with her? By mental telepathy?"

"No. By verbal telepathy on the telephone! Dr. Millstone gave me her private phone number and…."

"And? Don't tell me, Milka. You called her already behind my back and we're going to meet her next Saturday."

"Josip. Don't be stupid. Saturday is reserved for the weekly synagogue service."

"Thank God!"

"Thank God, indeed. She's coming instead to our apartment the very next day. On Sunday at 1:00 PM."

Josip bit his tongue and swallowed a tsunami of blasphemous words. He acceded to his wife's chicanery for only one reason…if God took Milka away from him, he would throw himself, feet first, into the nearest river and settle upon the bottom never to rise to the top.

FIFTY-TWO

The first light of day crept through his bedroom window and Josip's eyes responded to the wakeup call. The clock beside his bed informed him that he could sleep a little longer but his imagination dictated otherwise. "Who is this Lynn Van Praagh-Gratton?" he silently whispered to himself as Milka lay motionless next to him experiencing REM sleep. And then the brush of an artist started to paint a portrait in his mind of a woman who would visit once noon added an extra hour.

"I bet she's in her late twenties," Josip surmised. "Probably with long black curly hair that extended to her shoulders. Eyes as black as night with lids and eyelashes to match. A red bandana scarf on her head and large gaudy round earrings the size of plums. Yes, and some type of talisman around her neck and gold bangles on each wrist." Then his fantasy advanced further.

"A low cut revealing white silk blouse. A black sash around her waist. A multi-colored skirt that fluttered when she walked. Shoes? No! Boots. Black…laced high up her calf with spiked heels six inches high. And an accent? European and difficult to separate her words. Carrying a bag of tricks…coins…playing cards…strange powders concealed in leather pouches."

A yawn from Milka foiled further attempts to identify the invited guest who had been born with a gift that defied explanation.

"Are you up, Josip?" sighed Milka.

"Up, but unprepared. How could I have been so foolish as to let you talk me into trespassing into the unknown?"

Touching her husband's cheek with the tips of her fingers, Milka replied: "For two reasons. First, because you love me. Second, because we need to try to reach out to our son for his sake and for ours."

◆

The stairs were winding and steep but she finally reached the Weiss' fourth-floor walk-up tenement apartment on Orchard Street in Manhattan's Lower East Side. A knock on the door signaled her arrival and, standing on the other side of the entry, was a hand poised to let her in. Hesitating for a moment, Josip recalled the young woman who had introduced herself once he had awakened in bed hours earlier. "Let's see if I'm psychic," he challenged his reasoning. And once the door was fully opened and Lynn Van Praagh-Gratton stepped through the threshold, Josip realized that he had chosen the right profession....haberdashery rather than fortune-telling.

Milka rushed to greet her visitor with eyes opened wide and a heart beating as fast as a marathon runner approaching the finish line. At first glance, Milka judged Lynn to be in her middle to late thirties. Her appearance was that of "a very sweet lady who would blend into a crowd without people turning heads," she would later confide to her husband.

"Welcome to our home," voiced Josip in a modulated tone feeling embarrassed by the image that had started his day.

"Please take off your coat and treat our home as your home," exclaimed Milka with the broadest smile painting her face.

"Thank you," muttered Lynn as she was still restoring oxygen to exhausted lungs.

"Would you like a cold drink or a hot cup of tea?" queried a hostess aiming to please.

"No, Mrs. Weiss. Maybe later. Not at this very moment."

"I thought that we could sit around our small dining room table meant to seat four but more comfortable for three," urged Josip.

"That would be fine with me," was Lynn's accommodating words.

And each took a seat as silence introduced a short respite before the psychic-medium plied her trade and shared her gift.

"You came highly recommended by Dr. Millstone," were Milka's reassuring words to build confidence and acceptance preceding the reading.

"He's a fine doctor and an even finer gentleman," replied Lynn Van Praagh-Gratton.

"Have you known him long?" was Josip's probing inquiry.

"Just over three years. He has referred a number of clients to me and I'm pleased to say that Milton, I mean Dr. Millstone, has been most appreciative for my healing work."

"I have come to learn that you have done several readings for Dr. Millstone personally," remarked Josip who still questioned whether anyone really had the ability to communicate with the dead.

"Yes, but my readings are privileged. I value each client's privacy like a lawyer or a clergyman clings to confidentiality."

"I understand completely," piped Milka hoping that the same courtesy would be extended to their reading.

"I don't mean to be rude or impolite," began Josip's expression of skepticism. "But, how do we know that what you do is real and what you say has not been delivered by a colorful imagination?"

The question caused Milka to cringe, fearing that Lynn would receive the remark as an insulting jab at her integrity. But, to the contrary, the psychic-medium welcomed the opportunity to establish her credentials and to demonstrate credibility.

"Know, at the start, that I know nothing about what I presume was a loss in your lives. Were it not for a death, recent or distant, there would be no need for me to sit in this chair. When Mrs. Weiss called to make an appointment, I cautioned her not to provide any information to me so that my reading would be pristine and untainted. Also, be assured that I have not spoken to Dr. Millstone about you or your yearning to communicate to a place that I call *Beyond the Beyond* where energies reside when they leave this earthly plane. If you doubt my word, a call to the good doctor can easily set your minds at ease once he returns to his office tomorrow."

"We don't doubt your sincerity and honesty," chimed Josip. "But, is it possible for you to tell us about yourself, your gift, and your beliefs before the reading begins? It will be most helpful if you could elaborate since the world is filled with those claiming to have a gift when they really don't."

"What you ask fills me with pleasure since recounting my life story brings back memories that even amaze me to this day. Would you like the short, moderate, or long version? I have dedicated this afternoon completely to your desires. The modest fee for my services takes no account of time well spent."

"The long version," proclaimed Milka. "To be honest, my husband needs to be convinced that God blessed you with a unique gift which most don't experience."

"I am a Doubting Thomas to be sure," confirmed Josip. "But, I'll keep an open mind and a receptive heart hoping to witness your celebrated powers."

"That's all that I ask," encouraged Lynn. "The more open you are…the more you attract a departed energy to speak through me. Comfort will come with knowing who I am. My life story."

"The long version of your life story?"

"Yes, Mr. Weiss. The long version if it pleases you."

"It pleases me, indeed," replied a Doubting Thomas.

"My mother, Regina ("Jean") F. McLane, and my father, Allan L. Van Praagh, were married in Manhattan, New York; she, age 29, and he, four years her junior. For a time, my mother worked for Walt Disney Productions in New York City as, believe it or not, Walt Disney's private secretary!

"My father's side of the family traced their lineage to those speaking Dutch with a sprinkling of Welsh mixed in for good measure. My mother, by contrast, had roots honoring the Irish and their marvelous heritage.

"For my mother, religion was the linchpin of her life having been raised in a strict Irish Catholic household. Dutifully, she carried these traditions in her mind and in her heart and applied them to our day-to-day lives. With a powerful connection to the Blessed Mother Mary, and especially to St. Thérèse of Lisieux, popularly called 'The Little Flower of Jesus' or just 'The Little Flower,' my mother embraced religion with an inexhaustible passion.

"Throughout her adult life, my mother cast her eyes skyward beseeching the heavenly Little Flower of Jesus to help her cope with mounting times of despair. Sadly, despondency often intruded into my mother's life, stalking her with all the ferocity of a lion on the prowl desperate for a meal. Like a medicinal elixir intended to comfort an aching heart, Regina Van Praagh would tutor: 'If you ever feel alone or need help, then offer this prayer to St. Thérèse…*Little Flower in this hour, please show your power*.' In the same spirit of acceptance, I too grew to love the imagery of one who sacrificed much to help others and, as a testament to my own personal devotion and commitment, I proudly took Thérèse's name as my confirmation name.

"While mother was a devout Catholic, my father was raised as an Episcopalian which did not sit well with my mother. In her mind, if you swayed an inch from her chosen faith then you might as well be a heathen. This religious difference would be a smoldering cauldron of tension sitting on our family hearth throughout my upbringing.

"When my father exchanged marriage vows, he came to the marriage with the grandest hopes, dreams, and ambitions. Like 'The Little Flower,' he chose service to his community, donning the uniform of a New York City police officer. But, fate was unkind to his desires. Diagnosed with type 1 diabetes two years after joining the force, the stress of the job played havoc with his disease and the predicated long-term consequences to his health became painfully real. Thus, my father surrendered to necessity and traded his dress blues for less formal attire and a different form of 'less stressful' excitement. He became a stagehand for television and Broadway productions."

"How exciting!" exclaimed Milka, momentarily interrupting Lynn before she continued.

"During the course of his work, my father met scores and scores of celebrities and stars in the making. I could go on and on and on describing his encounters with so many differing personalities whose emotions ran the gamut…sad, happy, whimsical, humorous, and, occasionally, tragic.

"Although Allan L. Van Praagh, my beloved father, was thrown off life's intended path by a serious genetic health issue, I am proud to recall that he never complained or bemoaned what might have been judged to be fate's cruel injustice. He confronted life with reborn perseverance.

"Wishes and expectations were not so easily fulfilled for Regina and Allan and, as time marched along, they voiced a growing concern. They wanted to celebrate the arrival of a firstborn, but somehow nature was resistant refusing to cooperate. So, my mother sought a physician's opinion, and, after a pelvic examination, his answer was disquieting. The haunting diagnosis was a 'retroverted uterus,' or 'tipped uterus,' which occurs when the uterus is tipped backwards towards the spine. In the vast number of cases reported, the cause has its origin in genetics.

"According to my mother, the doctor offered a grim assessment for her chances of conceiving a child. In his words, denied of compassion, he said: 'The condition that I have found Mrs. Van Praagh is most uncommon.

Likely, you'll never conceive a child.' His advice: 'Try sitting in hot baths to see if the abnormality improves.'

"The advancement of science and medicine has been astounding but, at the time, few options were available to my mother to correct the condition and to welcome the arrival of a healthy fetus. So, what did my mother do? Night after night after night she soaked in a hot bath praying to St. Thérèse of Lisieux to send a beating heart to her womb. And her prayers were finally answered months later.

"What an extraordinary woman my mother was to persist and persist and persist unwilling to surrender to the doctor's bleak prediction. For that perseverance, I express gratitude sketched by the most vibrant colors of the rainbow.

"Confirming what she had already sensed— that she was incubating a precious life— my mother again consulted her physician who confirmed her self-diagnosis. Again, however, he would prove to be wrong. 'The baby will come on our nation's birthday….July 4th,' he said with a renewed reassurance. Well, I didn't cooperate. It was June 29th when my loving parents held me in their arms for the very first time. And, thereafter, three siblings followed in succession, eventually expanding our family to six.

"Thus, just as summer replaced spring, Lynn Elizabeth, (me!), was joined with the Van Praagh surname. I don't know why my parents chose Lynn, but I suspect that it relates to my father's sprinkling of Welsh in his bloodline. You see, Lynn is an English family name which is derived from Welsh "llyn lake." As for Elizabeth, it honors my paternal grandmother, Ethel Burrows-Van Praagh, who was English. Therefore, my middle name pays tribute to the Queen of England. But, believe you me, royalty I'm not!

"Since the day I was born, I have lived an unpretentious life without a driving urge prodded by materiality. Growing up, my family shared a modest two-family home in Bayside, Queens, New York, with relatives. Our clan occupied the upstairs quarters while my Aunt Catherine and my Uncle Stubby, a delightful nickname, were content to be nesting downstairs. These humble surroundings, you need to know, enriched my life with middle-class values which have helped to mold and to shape the woman who I have become.

"Let me pause for a moment to be upfront with you both. I don't have all the answers to the most important question that we, as humans, yearn to know…What is the meaning of existence? To fill in some of the blanks, I am sharing my life experiences which I hope will be instructive or even mind-changing. Like you, I am yearning to know more. And, as my days have blended into months and then years, I have grown in understanding thanks to a generous gift that allows me to communicate *Beyond the Beyond* which inspires me.

"My experience as a psychic-medium has taught me that the essence of creation, as well as the essence of being, is something that we oft-times take for granted...***LIGHT***! And what feeds the energy of light to strengthen its transformative power?...***LOVE***!

"The message that has been channeled by my psychic awareness throughout my life, gleaned from what I call 'the universal *Source* of knowledge,' is that to try to glimpse into the meaning of life we must gain a greater understanding of light. This path, I firmly believe, will lead, pardon the pun, to eternal "enLIGHTenment."

"From ancient scriptures to modern scientific discoveries, light has played a featured role. The ancients informed us in *Genesis 1:3* that on the first day of creation God said: 'Let there be light.' And centuries later, Albert Einstein incorporated the concept of light into the most famous equation ever penned...$E=mc^2$...when explaining the relationship between mass and energy. [c representing the speed of light in a vacuum and telling us that energy equals mass multiplied by the speed of light squared.]

"So, let me share my first memories of being blessed with a psychic gift. And what delivered that message? ***LIGHT***!

"For the most part, childhood memories that advance way back in time tend to be few for most of us, unless, of course, they leave what Thoreau called a 'mindprint.' And I can recall, with all the vividness of it occurring yesterday, such a transformative event in my life when I barely crept past my third birthday.

"My family was having dinner with my Aunt Catherine and my Uncle Stubby in our home in Bayside, Queens, New York. The air was so thick it could be sliced with a proverbial knife, and black foreboding clouds promised an arriving summer storm. And then it came, thunder and lightning that rattled our windows and teased and tested our emotions.

"Reliving the experience, I remember being a frightened child as the storm introduced its fury. The thunder claps terrorized me, and I'm sure that my little body must have been quaking and quivering at the time because I recall that my Uncle Stubby placed me on his knee by a window overlooking our small grassy backyard and embraced me to provide comforting reassurance.

"And then it happened! A blinding lightning bolt slammed into the ground outside that picture window and an odd sensation consumed my emotions. I know this seems strange, even bizarre, but I assure you it was so real that the memory has attached itself to me like a haunting shadow. The light that violently exploded before my eyes made me feel as though it had 'traveled through me.' And then...and then...I sensed, or somehow knew, that there had been some sort of shapeless form in the flash of light the moment that it struck the ground. In retrospect, I would describe the figure as 'translucent without gender.'

"How did that day alter my life? With a mixture of both joy and fear, if the truth be told. Since that day, I carry within my psyche an aching anxiety about thunder and lightning. I guess most people do, especially young children who have had early memories of an event that proved to be traumatic. But, strangely, while I fear the ferocity of thunder and lightning, I have also grown to love it as well. Why? Because that early childhood event changed my life, not for a fleeting moment but rather for forever! It somehow tutored that in light there is love and some deeper celestial meaning, perhaps leading to a pathway to *Beyond the Beyond*."

"That's amazing!" interrupted Milka for a second time craving to know more.

"Did I mention this event at the time to Uncle Stubby, or years later to anyone else?" continued Lynn. "No! Why? I believe it was out of an innate fear of being disbelieved or, far worse, being misjudged and labeled with an unkind adjective.

"Two years later, at age five, our family traveled 313 miles upstate to Dansville, New York, during the summer, for a short vacation to spend time with our extended family—my maternal grandmother, Katherine D. McLane, and cousins. Dansville, a sleepy little village in the eastern part of Livingston County, got its name from Daniel Faulkner who settled in the area in 1795. No doubt the village's greatest claim to fame is that Millard Fillmore, our 13th President, resided in Dansville for several months.

"In an upstairs bedroom, my cousin, Ruth, and I were playing as a light rain began to fall. Suddenly, like an unexpected stranger banging on the door to shock those tending to their business inside, an electrifying ball of lightning struck the ground in front of the house. The sky lit up like a Fourth of July fireworks celebration and the house rumbled. Quickly, my eyes were drawn to the window and, once again, I perceived a shapeless specter in the pillar of light. Vividly, I remember asking my cousin whether she had seen what I had seen. Her reply was 'No!' And, for a child of five, the lack of confirmation was unnerving. 'What's wrong with me?' I questioned. Thereafter, apprehension intruded into my life and I decided to keep my observations quietly to myself.

"In addition to having relatives living in Dansville, New York, I also had cousins residing in Rochester, New York. When our family visited them, I slept in a room that had a maroon rocking chair that had been passed down from generation to generation, originally belonging to my great-grandmother, my mother's mother, Katherine, who had long since passed to the other side. Strangely, each time I visited Rochester, and each time I slept in the same bedroom, out of nowhere, the rocker would begin to sway back and forth. Was I frightened? Surprisingly not! Something within my heart of hearts reached deep into the fiber of my being and told me to be still and to feel peacefully at ease. Why were my emotions composed and tranquil? Because, from *Beyond the Beyond*, the energy of my deceased Great-Aunt Maggie O' Day had come to pay me a visit and, as a child, I somehow received her presence with a soothing calm.

"Josip. Still skeptical? You have a right to be. But, we started our journey together exchanging trust, and please accept what I am about to describe with uninhibited confidence. Why? Because I will never compromise my integrity by exaggerating, or worse yet, by lying. To do so would discredit my gift in your eyes, stain my reputation for the balance of my life, and negate my healing work!

"My Great-Aunt Maggie was a gifted psychic, a trait that blazes a path straight through my mother's lineage. Not to jump too far ahead, let me just say that my mother had the gift. I have the gift. My youngest brother was blessed with the gift. And, my firstborn son, Dennis, is gifted as well. But, back to Great-Aunt Maggie and the rocker.

"I saw a white mist enveloping an image of Maggie as the chair rocked back and forth. Looking back, I believe that it was an energized haze of purified light. While the images in my two recounted lightning experiences were free of bodily details, not so with my departed aunt. From that day to this, her sculpted likeness, sitting in the rocker, is emblazoned on my memory.

"What I saw, with clarity of vision, was a woman of middle-age. She wore a high-collared long dress and her hair was neatly wrapped in a bun. It was Maggie all right. And, I have not a shred of lingering doubt!

"I shared this experience with my cousins and only a few close relatives. Looking back with hindsight, they probably chalked it up to a young child's actively creative imagination. Nothing more. But, I assure you…I know what I saw, and the stunning memory has been securely stored away forever in the filing cabinet of my mind. And, I'm pleased to have retrieved it now so that I can share it with you.

"Continuing, Rochester and Dansville are relatively close in proximity, only separated by 56 miles. So, when we left the former where I was visited by my great-aunt from *Beyond the Beyond*, we stopped in Dansville for a short visit. It was good to once again spend time with my maternal grandmother, Katherine D. McLane, and my cousin, even if the visit was intended to be abbreviated.

"That night, I had a dream. I saw my grandmother, Katherine, rocking in the maroon chair that I had just seen the spirit of my Great-Aunt Maggie occupy. At the time, as a very young child, I made no sense of the message that was being delivered from *Beyond the Beyond*. In retrospect, the imagery is haunting—a premonition of something tragic to come! And two weeks later after returning home? We had to hastily return to Dansville because Katherine had unexpectedly died of a heart attack!

"While it is unusual in contemporary times to hold a wake in a family's residence, at that time, it was a common practice in a number of very religious households. And, as a five-year-old, the fact that my grandmother's coffin occupied space in the living room parlor downstairs awaiting burial did not register as being odd in my brain. Like most children, lacking the maturity offered by experience, I accepted it as the norm.

"Grandmother's coffin had been placed directly beneath the bedroom I was sleeping in. Did I, a child of little more than 60 months, understand the concept of death at the time? Probably only with a modest degree of awareness shrouded in vagueness. That's why what happened next confounded me.

"Sure, Grandma Katherine's body was at rest below my bedroom; but…but…I keenly felt her presence in my room upstairs accompanied by a pervasive musty smell which I had always identified as hers. Was I frightened? Strangely not because I sensed that she was conveying love to me. It's impossible to describe, but I just knew that she was surrounded by, and offering me, her love. And then my mind received a further message of comforting reassurance from her which told me that she was 'at peace' and really 'all right.' To say I was perplexed and bewildered at the time is to understate the obvious.

"'How can grandma be downstairs and upstairs at the same time?' my tiny brain yearned to know. 'It must be magic,' I recall saying to myself. So, what did I do? What most children of five would probably do instinctively. In the middle of night, when everyone was fast asleep, I crept downstairs to the coffin to see if grandma was still there. Well, of course she was, which toyed with my emotions and my perception of reality.

"That night, shortly after falling asleep, my grandmother came to me in a dream. In it, and again I remember the memory as clearly as if it had been tape recorded, I heard Katherine's voice telling me: 'I'm in a most beautiful place. I'm home for sure.'

"How can a child process the event I have just described? Panic? Fear? Bewilderment? Well, for me, I was composed and accepting. I felt the presence of my grandmother to be a precious gift. Why? Because I believed, no I knew, that somehow she was still with me and connected to my life. Her body had failed her, but the richness of her love endured and nestled in my heart!

"I wanted to share my experience with my family, but something or someone from *Beyond the Beyond* cautioned a child of five to conceal it from others. In looking back, I'm glad to have accommodated that voice of wisdom for surely I would have been labeled 'weird' or, even worse, 'crazy.'

"What I'm about to share with you tugs at my heartstrings and requires that I take a deep breath and wipe away more than one tear from my cheek. As I mentioned earlier, the gift, and I truly recognize it as a 'healing' gift intended to bring solace to others, has its genesis, for me and my youngest brother, on my mother's side of the family. And my mother, Regina, was part of an unbroken chain linking one generation to another generation to yet another generation.

"While my brother and I have mastered the art of being a psychic-medium and accepted the gift with a generous spirit once we grew to understand its power and purpose, my mother struggled with the notion that those residing *Beyond the Beyond* begged that she have a receptive ear for their words. For mom, the sense of energy, or spirits around her, sent shockwaves through her psyche. Unlike today when spirituality has opened many doorways into what I call 'the possible,' during my mother's tender years, one would have been ostracized if he or she suggested, for an instant, that he or she had been visited by one whose flesh had been long ago laid to rest.

"For my mother, torment followed her throughout her life since she could not begin to comprehend why she was sensing things and hearing things that her peers were not privy to. In order to cope with what she thought to be a plaguing illness, or perhaps a curse conjured up by the biblical Devil, she turned first to her religion and then, ultimately, to a more potent elixir.

"Tragically, my mom became an alcoholic and, sorrowfully, whiskey never was able to anesthetize her aching heart. As a result, the normality of our family's life was shredded. And who carried the heaviest burden wrought by my mother's lack of sobriety? Me!

"My mother was raised a strict Irish Catholic and she greeted each Sunday as a day of celebration and, more often than not, a day of sobriety when a family could actually function as nature had intended. Attending church was not simply a driving necessity fostered by repetitive tradition. No! To Regina F. McLane-Van Praagh, it fulfilled a need as important as feeding a restless stomach. We children were sent to parochial school to perfect our faith and we accompanied our mother to mass each and every Sunday. The only one excused was our father who attended, when he wished, another church in keeping with his Episcopalian upbringing.

"In the early years, I can recall attending 12:30 PM church services with my mother and my brother, Michael. As young children, we were fidgety and lacking patience during what proved to be a lengthy mass. By the time we reached the consecration, which literally means 'association with the sacred,' my brother and I were inclined to drift back in order to relax our backs. But, our mother would have none of what she viewed as disrespect. 'Kneel up! Kneel up!' she would whisper in a voice just loud enough to gain our attention and our compliance. 'Kneel up! Kneel up!' still rings in my ears.

"Not satisfied with our educational training at Catholic school…not sufficiently pleased with our religious exposure on Sundays at church…my mother made us sit and watch what seemed like endless movies that carried a religious theme and divine message. She was particularly drawn to the Blessed Mother Mary and, as mentioned earlier, St. Thérèse of Lisieux, 'The Little Flower.' But no amount of devotion and prayer could arrest the demons that haunted my mother's state of mind. The psychic gift of receiving messages and visitations from *Beyond the Beyond* tampered with her will to live and her only recourse was to deaden her emotions with a bottle of whiskey poured into glass after glass Monday through Saturday.

"So, what becomes of the family unit when a mother is an alcoholic and the breadwinner is hardly home at night because he is a stagehand for television and Broadway productions? The answer is that many of the domestic responsibilities are bequeathed to the eldest child of the family, especially if she is a girl. And, the firstborn Van Praagh child was I.

"I well up with painful emotions when I recall that I never had a real childhood because I never had a supportive mother. After age 10, for all intents and purposes, I was the mom with my mother frequently inebriated and my dad working what, by that time, had become two jobs. All I yearned for was to come home from school and smell dinner cooking on the stove. More times than not, that task was left to me.

"I couldn't bring friends home for fear that my mother was drunk and that nasty gossip back at school would spread like a wildfire gone out of control. If the truth be told, I freely admit that I was jealous of my friends who lived a 'normal' life with loving and doting parents who spent quality time with them, bought them toys, and took them on adventurous vacations.

"Quite often after returning home from school, I would find that my mother was sprawled on the floor with blood gushing from her head. It was the alcohol, of course. She had consumed so much that she had lost her equilibrium. What was I to do? Times too many to count, I had to call my neighbor Mrs. Clark, or my father, or even the police. Leaving school, I never knew what to expect once I opened the front door. It was heart-wrenching and downright terrorizing!

"Let me preface my next recollection with the message that I love my siblings. One day, I came home from school and my mother was, believe it or not, sober. And, I could tell that she was excited to tell me something that she judged to be extremely important. 'Had she decided to stop drinking for good?' That would have been more exhilarating than opening presents on Christmas Day, though presents were few in our household and our stockings received only a Clementine orange, which I loath to this day. Anyway, doing away with the liquor bottle was not on her mind. To my chagrin, she said in a message that reverberates in my ears to this day: 'I'm going to have another baby.' To repeat again…I love my siblings. However, at the time, my only thought was…'How can you have another child when you can't take care of the ones you already have?'

"Frequently, I was forlorn as a child. And, the fact that my father would fight with my mother because of her addiction added another layer of stress upon my tiny shoulders and my impressionistic mind. How did I cope? To relieve my anxiety, I invariably raced to our backyard and climbed an apple tree to just escape from a sad and complicated reality. As an adult, I now understand the symbolism. The tree was planted deep into the ground encouraging my psyche also to try to become grounded!

"As time advanced, nothing really changed. My two brothers, my sister, and I had absentee parents. And yes, as the eldest, much fell upon me. I became the 'Little Mommy' assigning household tasks to my siblings, overseeing their homework assignments, enforcing bedtime hours, and expressing heartfelt concern for their well-being. I had little time for personal time with friends. The only time when my emotions were rescued for a fleeting moment was on Sundays when my mother would suspend drinking to attend to God's work...church and preparing a proper family dinner to give thanks to God. And Sunday proved even more glorious because our father was able to take time off from work and spend time with all of us. I felt as though I had a real dad and mom, just like everyone else.

"But reality returned once Monday replaced Sunday. Regrettably, one-seventh of a week does not a week make. And, there are lessons here to be conveyed with an earnest heart... starting with family bonds trump everything...followed by unhealed wounds scar one's psyche for life... and, finally, forgiveness can be difficult or sometimes nearly impossible, but lingering resentment slowly eats away at the tissue of one's heart.

"I could be angry at my mother for abandoning her duties as a mother and sweeping them in my direction. But I realize that a psychic gift is a coin with two sides. It can be a blessing or a curse.

"Grappling with being a psychic-medium was just too much for my mother to grasp and to grow to accept. She struggled to make sense of it, and failing to do so, it clearly got the better of her. Sometimes a blessing when not properly understood can become as destructive as an incurable disease!"

"Do you ever have premonitions?" asked Milka caught in the grasp of Lynn's narrative.

"Yes. And your question coincides with the next story I'm about to share."

"Please continue," insisted Josip.

"It was an exciting time in my life when the focus of my dysfunctional family paused for a fraction of a moment to channel all of its positive energy to me when I was to be confirmed in my mother's church. And, I couldn't constrain my joy for a single minute. The anticipation was building in my chest like a balloon being filled with helium. And, I was just as buoyant as that object once it was released to float skyward.

"Confirmation is one of the seven sacraments that sketches the religious upbringing of a devoted Catholic. Its significance lies in the fact that according to doctrine, by receiving confirmation, one is sealed with the gift of the Holy Spirit and strengthened in one's Christian life and beliefs.

"Rising early to prepare for the ceremony, my mother insisted that the family, mother and kids, pile into the car to go to a local jewelry store so that she could buy me a gift to commemorate the celebratory occasion. Rarely did I get a present. So, this day promised to be a magical moment in my life.

"We had left plenty of time to return home in order to properly dress in more formal attire for the afternoon service. Ready to leave, my brother Michael was the last to arrive running hastily to the car. What caused his delay would become all too apparent, and all too disquieting, later on.

"As we approached the jewelry store, my heart skipped a beat and then another and yet another. It was a fire engine blaring its siren to alert drivers to yield the right of way. 'Mom,' I said. 'I think our house is on fire.' And, I could see in my mind's eye firemen spraying water from their hoses all over our house. My mother's reply was: 'Stop that crazy thinking!' So, I silenced my tongue, but couldn't quell my concern.

"After buying me a decorative pin in the shape of an ornate spoon, we returned home to relax and then dress for my confirmation. As we turned onto my street, black smoke billowed in the air and I knew that my premonition had been real, not imagined. Was I right?

"Once my mother hit the brakes in front of our house, we all gasped in disbelief. A raging fire had engulfed the roof. Without thinking, remember I was an innocent child, I leapt out of the car. Because? I needed to rescue my beautiful gown that my mother had bought just for the confirmation ceremony. Before I could reach the door, a fireman luckily grabbed me and told me that I couldn't go in. When I explained the urgency, he promised to save my dress. What a hero in my mind.

"Someone must have called my father at work for soon he showed up. With tears gushing in my eyes, I feared that all of my possessions, though they were few in number, had probably been destroyed by fire, water, and/or soot since my bedroom was upstairs below the fiery roof. 'Don't cry,' insisted my father. 'The most important thing is that we are all safe.' But, I still couldn't get my emotions settled because my confirmation promised to be the most important day in my life.

"Putting the blaze out rather quickly, the firemen saved our house from total destruction. Thereafter, while it was being repaired, we stayed in a local motel for weeks. And my precious dress? True to his assurance, the fireman was able to put out the blaze before it reached my closet and thus it was saved, except for one minor imperfection…its aroma!

"Even though my dress smelled of smoke, I wore it with a smile laced on my face. As I look back, I can't help but chuckle because I vividly remember that kids attending the service begged me to let them smell the dress. They were intrigued by its scent and the story attached to it.

"The gift of the Holy Spirit that I received that day filled me with such elation that I put the fire completely out of my head. Fittingly, the bishop remarked that I was 'a strong young lady who could overcome anything.' And, I carry the vitality of that message in my heart to this very day.

"And the cause of the fire? Remember that Michael was hurriedly running from the house to the car just before we left for the jewelry store? Well, my brother, who by this time had already well-cemented a reputation for being both rebellious and mischievous, had lit a match while horsing around and ignited a mattress stored in a closest!"

"How horrible!" lamented Milka visualizing the day's events.

"Since then, I've had countless premonitions that have visited my waking and sleeping hours from then until now."

"What about dreams? Can they tell a story about the future?" questioned Josip.

"Indeed, let me recount one that has stuck in my memory."

"Please share it with us," pleaded Milka.

"Our family decided to take a break from the congestion of the suburbs, leaving the stale air behind. It was a summer vacation in the Berkshire Mountains in Massachusetts that sent my twelve-year-old heart aflutter. Hiking, swimming, and camping whet my appetite for excitement like the advance of Christmas Day.

"Laying my head on my pillow two nights before the engine of our car would begin to hum, I fell into a deep sleep. And then happiness was quickly wrestled away from me like a thief carrying off my precious belongings. A foreboding dream warned that something dreadful would happen on our trip, and the culprits were water and my right foot. And… and…while playing in a creek after we had settled in, I cut…you guessed it…my right foot on a piece of glass spoiling my fun for the entire trip."

"How awful," exclaimed Milka imagining the pain. "How could you have foreseen an injury to your right foot in water days before it happened?"

"Because she is blessed with a gift," admitted Josip whose impression of Lynn was beginning to change from non-believing to believing.

"Lynn, are you married? Do you have children?" was Milka's burning desire to know.

"Milka, do you believe in stories of love at first sight?"

"Yes, Josip and I did fall in love at first sight."

"And Milka, so did I."

"Please tell me how it happened to you," insisted Josip's beaming wife.

"While most are blessed with 'soulful' mates, a privilege few are blessed with 'soul' mates, a union of two hearts that beat rhythmically as one.

"It was a warm summer's day in July. While most children my age were playing in the park or swimming laps in a pool or splashing in the Atlantic Ocean, I was trekking off to summer school at Flushing High School to make up for a deficiency in my English studies during my freshman year. Seated beside my girlfriend, Michelle, who also was making up for an undernourished grade, I spotted a boy on the bus who immediately caught my eye. And I said silently to myself, 'I know one day we're going to be together.' Had someone from *Beyond the Beyond* whispered that message in my ear? I'll let you be the judge once I complete my story about Dennis.

"Somehow, I knew that this unnamed boy and I were destined to meet again, and several bus rides later there he was again. Too shy to introduce myself, I just asked those residing *Beyond the Beyond* to keep an eye on him for me until fate brought us together.

"Well, summer blended into fall and I was back in high school resuming studies during my sophomore year. The school had a liberal policy when it came to breaks between classes, which were called 'open periods.' The administration allowed us to leave the building to retrieve a bit of fresh air. So, during a lull in classes, several girlfriends asked if I wanted to go to the park to watch the boys play basketball. My mind didn't tell me to go, my body did. I felt as though I was being pulled towards the door. Were those dwelling *Beyond the Beyond* tampering with destiny?

"As I approached the court with my classmates, there he was! The boy who had captured my attention on the summer school bus. My legs grew wobbly and I nearly lost my balance—as well as my composure. Let me interrupt for a moment to mention the word 'manifestation.'

"'Manifestation' is the act of willing something. You visualize it in your mind's eye and you capture and channel your internal energy and direct it to achieving or fulfilling your desire. For me, that was something that often occurred in my life. So, I questioned whether I had 'manifested' meeting the young boy again. Although an answer never arrived to provide conclusive evidence one way or the other, I'd like to think that my obsession with a boy named Dennis was a 'wish fulfilled.'

"As I and my girlfriends moved closer to the court, the boys paused their game for a moment to welcome our visit. One of the girls seemed to know most of the boys and took charge of introducing everyone. And then my pulse picked up speed like a racehorse sprinting to the finish line. 'Dennis, this is Lynn,' said Rachel. It seems that she and Dennis knew one another since they lived on the same block. What a coincidence! Well, Dennis politely came over to me and we chatted for awhile. Before returning to school to continue my classes, my heart told my mind: 'You're going to marry this boy.' Was it love at first sight once I spotted him on the bus for the very first time? Yes! 'Soul mates to spend a lifetime together?' Yes! At age fifteen, I had gleaned the answer 'yes' twice expressed and beamed with joy.

"Little did I know at that very moment, Dennis had also envisioned a life spent with me. Let me share a secret. The first blush of romantic love is the purest form of perfection whose song serenades the universe!

"Desperate to connect with Dennis, I hung around the basketball court after school but he was nowhere to be seen. When I felt the need to satisfy a spiritual urging during my adolescent years, I oft-times called upon by departed Aunt Maggie to provide guidance. And, when my mind set about to challenge my longing for Dennis, Aunt Maggie would say to me: 'Be patient. He will come back in due time.'

"Days stretched into a week and my pining for Dennis escalated into intense desire. And then fate, or rather Rachel, came to the rescue. 'Do you want to go to the candy store in my neighborhood?' she asked. 'I think Dennis will be there.' Little did I know that my soul mate-to-be, Dennis, had put Rachel up to making the suggestion—wanting to see me as much as I wanted to see him. So, of course, I went and my Mr. Right was waiting patiently for me. Like an experienced matchmaker, Rachel again re-introduced me to Dennis and then darted off to allow NATURE to work HER magic. And, SHE cleverly infused love into our two hearts. From that moment on, we became an inseparable couple for life.

"One week after meeting at the candy store, Dennis and I were attending a party in the basement of Christine's house, a common friend. Timid and shy, I sat down and Dennis immediately came over and sat next to me. My heart nearly leapt out of my chest. Before I could barely form the word 'hello,' Dennis took my hand and slipped a small sapphire ring on my wedding finger. 'What are you doing?' I said with a confluence of wonder and joy. 'I want you to go steady with me!' he exclaimed. And a kiss on his cheek delivered my answer quickly. And a return kiss on mine by Dennis sealed our commitment.

"After the party ended, my Sir Galahad walked me to the city bus that would take us both back home. Just as the bus was pulling up to the curb to receive us, Dennis whispered: 'I'm going to marry you.' And, under a starlit night, my heart expressed the very same desire.

"From that day forward, Dennis and I seriously dated and our love blossomed with all the sensual beauty of a ruby red rose. Parties and dances confirmed what everyone already knew—that there was no keeping us apart.

"On a hot summer's day that bridged my junior and senior year of high school, Dennis and I were bored. So, on a lark, I asked him if he wanted to play with a Ouija board just for fun. And he said: 'OK.' I since realize that playing with a Ouija board is playing with fire. While the board might provide some insights into the future, it also has the power to attract negative energy that can be dangerously destructive. Anyone who has a board should dispose of it at once!

"Anyway, I asked the Ouija board whether Dennis and I were going to get married and it answered 'Yes.' My follow-up inquiry centered around 'when,' and it spelled out the month of 'October.' Four years later, in October, we did become engaged. Then curiosity took us to Dennis' career path and it said: 'Will retire as a detective in homicide.' This thought never had entered Dennis' mind. Did the answer ring true? As destiny would have it, Dennis did become a New York City police detective.

"Following graduation from high school, I mirrored my mother's career path at the start. Like she, I gained employment with Walt Disney Productions at their offices located in Manhattan. That lasted two years until I became pregnant. In later years to bring additional income to the family, I joined American Airlines as a manager of flight attendants.

"Dennis and I were eager to get married, but he hadn't as yet 'popped the question' as the expression tutors. One morning, Dennis called me to tell me that he and his brother, Gary, were taking Gary's boat out of the marina in Bayside, Queens, New York, for a leisurely ride on the water. Moments after we hung up, I had a foreboding warning coursing through my arteries. And, the psychic in me understood what was to come for three hours later Dennis called from a doctor's office. It seems that when the two brothers returned to shore, Dennis cut his foot badly when he jumped out of the boat onto the ramp landing onto a piece of broken glass just waiting to put a miserable footnote, (no pun intended), to what had been a glorious day. Stitches too numerous to count closed the wound, a pair of crutches became his companion for weeks to come, and he was told to try to keep off the foot as much as possible and to elevate his leg to aid the healing process.

"A week or so passed and I was returning home from work. It was a hot and sultry summer night and I recall perspiration dripping down my cheeks. Moments from the front door, I saw the strangest sight. Dennis was parked by the curb with his foot hanging out of the window. Why? Because he was heeding the doctor's advice about elevating his foot whenever he could. Well, that's my Dennis!

"'Get into the car,' Dennis insisted with a voice that was showing impatience. So, I hopped into the front seat and then he said something that threw me for a *loop*. 'We have to go to Greenwalds Jewelers in Flushing,' he said with an eagerness that couldn't be contained.

"Once we reached the jewelry store, Dennis told me to stay put. Struggling with the crutches, he awkwardly managed to reach the front door to usher himself in and then, shortly thereafter, he returned to the car trying to avoid placing his injured foot on the ground. 'What's going on?' I asked with bated anticipation dying to know. Silence was his answer prompted by a smile. The next thing I knew, he was taking me home.

"When we reached my house, Dennis pulled up to the curb and deadened the car's engine, and the mystery was answered. 'Don't get out of the car,' he insisted and, like a magician well-trained in the art of prestidigitation, he pulled a proverbial rabbit out of a hat, or, in this case, a small box from his pocket. Before a blush could color my excited face, Dennis asked: 'Will you marry me?' And my response? Well, as you can guess, the rest is history.

"The ring that adorned my finger had a small diamond, but the symbolism made the size much larger in my mind. We were soul mates determined by the force of the universe to be bathed in eternal love, not for a calendar lifetime but forever forged by the merger of limitless space and time!

"With the approval of two sets of families, our pledge of love looked forward to a wedding that was to be held at the Sacred Heart Church with a reception to follow at Burburans Hall. Everything was falling neatly into place since Dennis had just learned that he had passed the Police Officers' test and would immediately begin his training at the academy.

"As days blended into weeks, our big day was approaching with the intensity of a hurricane. Did I say hurricane? Believe it or not, days before we would exchange our vows the weather prognosticators were predicting a hurricane the day of our wedding. Yes, a full-fledged disastrous storm. Was I worried? No! I was terrified!

"The day before we were to be married, the skies turned dark…the winds began to howl…and the pitter patter of raindrops grew in volume and drenched the landscape. I remember walking to the hairdresser and saying to myself: 'This time tomorrow, I'll be married. I hope and pray.'

"Married during a hurricane? Could it be possible? Roads flooding…guests stranded…my limousine marooned on a flooded street… flower deliveries and food caterers thrown off schedule…raging winds and rains playing havoc with hair and dress clothes. It promised to be a collective disaster of disasters for a bride waiting years for her wondrously magical day to arrive.

"The night before the wedding, I can't tell you how much I focused all of my energies to send that storm out to sea. With howling winds and torrential rains beating on my windowpane, I tried to fall asleep to quiet my nerves. Tossing and turning like I was on a rocking ship on a stormy sea, I finally managed to drift into slumber land for a short while until the light of day peaked through my window.

"Well, fate proved to be generous to me starting the morning of my wedding. Whether it was prayers directed to the heavens…or those exercising influence from *Beyond the Beyond*…or just damn good luck…the rain and winds had vanished and hints of blue were starting to paint the sky. Gazing out of my window in thankful relief, I spotted a flower truck stopped by our house's curb and a man, carrying a beautiful bouquet of red roses, exited the vehicle and then made long strides to my door.

"Sent to me by Dennis hours before we were to become husband and wife, the note that accompanied his generous gesture of heartfelt affection simply said: '*I LOVE YOU*! Love Dennis.' It was a message that is still tucked away for safekeeping in my jewelry box at home, a constant reminder of our fidelity.

"With a disaster erased from the day, our wedding went off without a hitch. It proved to be a perfect afternoon that boasted tantalizing blue skies! I couldn't have asked for a better day in the breadth of my lifetime or, for that matter, a better partner in life to share it with!"

"What about children?" was Milka's excited question begging for a brisk answer.

"Two years after we were married, we welcomed a son into this world who was named after his doting father. Abundant joy filled our lives when little Dennis opened his eyes wide and we cradled him in our arms for the very first time. But the abiding happiness we felt was interrupted by tears when Dennis, Jr. was found to be jaundiced and had to be removed to an isolation room.

"'Why can't life flow easier?' I questioned aloud to Dennis, knowing the answer that: 'Struggles make us stronger and encourage us to appreciate the beneficent times in our lives!' Well, our little boy finally came home and three more siblings, (Gail Lynn, Christopher Gary, and Gregory Matthew), would eventually join him to make our house a loving home. Little did we know at the time that our firstborn would be blessed with a psychic gift that he had inherited from his grandmother and mother. Now a family of six, if the truth be told, it should have been seven. Why? Between pregnancy number 3 and 4, I had a miscarriage. Although the gender was never determined by testing, I know that the fetus was a girl. And please, take this on faith, I feel her presence around me at times.

"With a growing family—in physical size as well as in numbers—it was time to leave our Queens apartment and to find a home. At the urging of Dennis' brother Gary, we moved to Long Island less than a mile away from Gary's house. Dennis was as close to his brother as any brother could be. They not only shared a life together as police officers, they also shared the unbreakable bond of brotherly love deeply rooted in family. Sadly, fate intervened to sever that cord as Gary, in the springtime of his life, died tragically in a motorcycle accident. That day, I lost a dear… dear…dear brother-in-law. That day, Dennis lost a piece of his heart! Our third child, Christopher, now honors his uncle's memory with his name connected to his…Christopher Gary Gratton.

"I want to move on and tell you in detail about my gift, but I'd like to take a moment to tell you about my mother's passing since it strongly influenced my path in life."

"Please do. Please do," insisted Josip who awaited more convincing evidence of Lynn's powers as a psychic-medium.

"It started out as a lump in my mother's breast. In an era when medicine had not made strides to offer less invasive treatments, mastectomy was my mother's only recourse. And, she weathered the physical and emotional consequences like a trooper.

"My mother banished concerns and allowed them to drift away in order to quell the anxiety voiced and felt by others. Soon, she was back on her feet, but not for long. She experienced what the doctors called a 'mini-stroke' followed weeks later by a more devastating stroke which paralyzed the entire right side of her body. Tragically, she couldn't return home. Not then! Not ever! She was admitted to a rehabilitation center and then permanently transferred to a nursing home facility because she couldn't speak, walk, or control her right side. She remained there for five years until she passed through Eternity's Gate to *Beyond the Beyond*.

"When news arrived of my mom's passing in the home, I raced to the nursing facility. Standing by her bedside with my dad, I couldn't help but notice that she had the most amazing smile on her face. I kissed her on the cheek for one last time and softly whispered in her ear: 'Mommy, you are finally at rest. You never truly understood the gift that you were given, but I do. And I promise to use it for good to bring *love* and *peace* to those in need.' Strangely, I felt her energy above us looking down and trying to still our grief. It was an amazing sensation that still gives me the chills when I glance back in time.

"At her funeral, before her casket was closed, I saw light or energy surrounding her earthly remains. And, I closed my eyes and spoke to her telling her to journey to *Beyond the Beyond* on butterfly wings. At that moment, I vowed to honor her legacy by fully embracing her gift to me... the healing power that attaches to one who is a psychic-medium. And so, by helping others, I help myself to constantly refresh my memory of my mother!"

"How extraordinary," confessed Milka wiping tears from her eyes.

"Do you want to take a short break?" questioned Lynn.

"No. Let's continue so that you don't interrupt your fascinating story," declared Josip. "Tell us more about your gift. Speaking with those in a place you call *Beyond the Beyond*."

"For me, life has evolved, sending me on a journey of discovery as I advanced from childhood to adolescence and then into adulthood. Intuitively, I knew that I had a gift to share with others but, like a seed planted in the soil hidden from view, it took time to gather strength to pierce through a hidden veil and then fully blossom into something beautiful. I am still learning. I am still yearning to know more about myself and the reason why I was blessed with a unique gift that few are privileged to have. And, at times, quite unexpectedly, my book of life has advanced from one chapter to another chapter bringing new insights into my life. As my time on earth has lengthened, puzzle pieces, meaningless by themselves, have begun to form a coherent picture when paired with others.

"It had been my belief through my early formative years that I was traveling life's path without one special voice of inspiration to guide me. Certainly, family and friends were present to offer advice, solace, and, when needed, motivational direction. But an incorporeal or ethereal energy providing what we humans call intuition or wisdom to channel decision-making never crossed my mind until a family member and I embarked upon a cruise to visit ports in Europe. Little did I know when I boarded the ship that another destination would be added to my journey; the start of a sojourn that would allow me to rendezvous with my Spiritual Master Teacher.

"Aboard the vessel was a guest lecturer named Brian Leslie Weiss. Educated at Columbia University, and then earning a degree at Yale University School of Medicine, Brian eventually became Head of Psychiatry at Mount Sinai Medical Center in Miami, Florida. There, employing hypnosis as a tool to aid in delving into the mind of his patients to retrieve buried information that would assist him in the healing process, he discovered something quite astonishing. While under hypnosis, a patient named 'Catherine' began to relive past-life remembrances.

"Dr. Weiss never seriously entertained the idea of reincarnation before meeting Catherine. And, quite frankly, he was taken aback when she revisited the past. Intrigued, Brian Weiss set out to validate or to invalidate her story through an exhaustive examination of the public records. To his amazement, he discovered that her memories under hypnosis were just as she had recited. From that moment forward, Dr. Brian Weiss was persuaded that reincarnation was fact not fiction. Since then, he has consistently found that many phobias reported by his subjects have their genesis in past-life experiences. Fear of water was caused by a prior-life drowning. Discomfort by a high-collared blouse was evidenced by a past-life hanging. And, so on and so on. Thus, the experience with Catherine reshaped the doctor's ambition in life propelling a career devoted to researching 'reincarnation, past-life regression, future-life progression, and survival of the human soul after death.'

"So, back to the European cruise. It happens that Dr. Weiss was offering a past-life regression seminar and destiny, (or perhaps my Spiritual Master Teacher), led me to a chair to surrender to Brian Weiss' soothing voice. And…and…in no time, I was transported back in time to what I would later learn from digging into the historical record was December 29, 1890.

"In a regressive state, I clearly saw myself as a young boy, approximately 12 years of age. I was in the American West on an Indian reservation, later learning that it was the Lakota Pine Ridge Indian Reservation in South Dakota. I was a Native American.

"That past-life day, the air was thick with the stench of impending despair present as cavalry soldiers, dressed in their blue uniforms, rode swiftly onto the reservation. Why? History records to confiscate guns and rifles from the Lakota tribesmen. Experiencing the moment as vividly as though I were sitting in a movie theater watching a drama unfold, I saw the soldiers firing and killing men, women, and children. And then…and then…a bullet entered me and I was dead! Yes, I had been shot and killed. Strangely, my vision tutored that I had been mortally wounded that day, 126 years ago! How disturbing! How surreal!"

"Our child too had a past-life experience of death," blurted Josip unaware that he was feeding information to the psychic.

"Please, Mr. Weiss, don't provide information to me in advance of my reading. My mind must be clear and you must be assured that I'm not using your words and repeating them back to you."

"Lynn, I understand. Kindly continue where you left off," was Josip's reassuring message.

"Needless to say, the experience left me confused and alarmed. This was the first time that I had viewed myself living a past life, although instinctively I knew that my present life was just one of many. The vision that my mind absorbed was vivid and heart-wrenching, and it took more than a moment to digest its powerful message. I am, still to this day, living with the memory seared onto my visual consciousness.

"Upon reflection, I now know that the regression was intended to live with me well beyond the moment. 'But why?' I questioned myself. Time would be my ally and teach that it was meant to lead me to my Spiritual Master Teacher!

"Before moving forward, let me briefly tell you about the Wounded Knee Massacre, where I died, which occurred near Wounded Knee Creek on the Lakota Pine Ridge Indian Reservation.

"After the sun had barely risen on December 29, 1890, part of the 7th Cavalry Regiment led by Colonel James W. Forsyth entered the Lakota reservation to disarm the native people. A scuffle ensued with a deaf tribesman named 'Black Coyote' and then, the next thing that happened, soldiers began indiscriminately firing at Lakota men, women, and children. Some Indians retreated, claimed their weapons, and began firing back. But, it was futile, for the Indians were outnumbered and outgunned. Those Lakota who managed to survive fled. However, their desperate attempt to escape proved to be in vain as cavalrymen pursued and killed them even though many carried no arms.

"The dead totaled 299 Lakota and 25 soldiers. At the start, the reservation had been home to only 350 Native Americans: 230 men and 120 women and children. After the event, there were only 4 men and 47 women and children left to bury their dead and to mourn their loss.

"Following the Wounded Knee Massacre, 20 cavalrymen were the recipients of the Medal of Honor. The National Congress of American Indians petitioned the American government to rescind the awards. Their pleas fell on deaf ears. Today, the battlefield has been designated a National Historic Landmark."

"The treatment of the American Indians is a scar on the cherished history of this country," piped Milka.

"Along with the treatment of Black Americans," added Josip.

"To be sure. Inhumanity is a hallmark of the chronology of history since the dawn of civilization. But, returning to Dr. Weiss' regression. It allowed me to connect to the past so that I could make sense of the future. It wouldn't be long thereafter before I was introduced to my Spiritual Master Teacher!"

"Tell us about your Master Teacher," encouraged Josip, gaining confidence that Lynn was, as he would later describe to friends: "The real McCoy! A gifted psychic-medium."

"After the European cruise and the encounter with Dr. Weiss, a friend and I decided to vacation in South Dakota to see a part of the country which we felt would be scenically and historically inspiring. Oh yes…the fact that I carried the story of the Wounded Knee Massacre in my heart of hearts added weight to my decision to go. Our itinerary sketched out visits to Mount Rushmore, Custer State Park, the Wind Cave National Park, and more.

"Our flight was bound for Rapid City, South Dakota, known as the 'Gateway to the Black Hills,' but a terrible storm diverted us to Denver for an overnight stay. Checking into a local hotel, we lamented to the reservation clerk that our plans had been abruptly altered by the weather. As it turned out, the hotel employee became animated when we mentioned that one of our scenic stops would be the site of the Wounded Knee Massacre.

"The clerk then went on to tell us that she was half Native American and that her uncle, a Lakota, had been buried in a cemetery on the grounds of the Pine Ridge Reservation. After informing us of her uncle's name, the young lady asked if we would kindly 'check on the grave and take a picture.' How could we refuse? We couldn't!

"The atmosphere cleared the next morning and, in no time, the wheels of the plane touched down in Rapid City, South Dakota. As sight-seeing days blended, we eventually found ourselves at the Pine Ridge Reservation to tour the National Historic Landmark. Excusing myself, and then leaving my companion for several minutes, I was attracted to a fenced-in area, not knowing that it was the resting place of Chief Red Cloud, perhaps the most important leader of the Oglala Lakota. Slowly opening the gate, I proceeded to a bench by his grave where I seated myself to show respect and to close my eyes in contemplation. And then....

"Well, let me pause for a moment to introduce you to Chief Red Cloud. The diversion is purposeful for the greatness of the man cannot be blithely overlooked.

"A prominent leader of the Oglala Lakota, Red Cloud was born sometime in 1822 close to the forks of the Platte River, in close proximity to North Platte, Nebraska. He died at the age of 87 on December 10, 1909 on the Pine Ridge Reservation where he was buried.

"Admired and respected for his bravery and courage, Red Cloud fought to preserve Native American lands and their diminishing cultural heritage. A fierce warrior, between 1866 and 1868, he confronted the United States Army in a campaign that came to be known as 'Red Cloud's War' to defend Indian territorial rights in the Powder River Country in northeastern Wyoming and southern Montana. The Fetterman Fight or Massacre, (or the Battle of the Hundred Slain), proved to be Red Cloud's greatest triumph against the invading forces. It was the worst military defeat sustained by the U.S. Army on the Great Plains until the Battle of the Little Bighorn ten years later.

"In 1868, when Red Cloud's War concluded, the Chief signed the Treaty of Fort Laramie, which fashioned the Great Sioux Reservation, and 'he led his people in the important transition of reservation life.' Thereafter, Red Cloud made a number of trips to Washington, D.C. to lobby for better treatment of his clansmen, meeting personally with President Ulysses S. Grant and Commissioner of Indian Affairs Ely S. Parker.

"Buried on the Pine Ridge Reservation, Red Cloud was lauded as both a warrior and a diplomat trying to find common ground with the white man. Shortly before his death, he reportedly grieved:

'They made us many promises, more than I can remember.
But they kept but one—They promised to take our land…
And they took it.'

The United States Postal Service honored Chief Red Cloud posthumously
with a 10 cent Great Americans series postage stamp.

"Now back to my story. Sitting on a bench in front of a renowned
Native American hero, I felt a reverence that defies description. With eyes
closed, I heard the crying and soulful wailing of men, women, and
children. For an instant, I was unpredictably drawn back to the massacre at
Wounded Knee which I had experienced during my regression with Dr.
Weiss. Then, the anguishing chorus of voices subsided just as quickly as
they had arrived.

"I opened my eyes. The air was still, not a breeze to be felt that
entire day until a whisk of wind arose from nowhere and cleansed my face.
And then I felt an energy, his energy, envelope me like a father embracing a
child. And then…and then…I heard the timbre of his voice and these soothing
words spoken with the beauty of feeling: 'You are safe my child. I will always
be with you and protect you into eternity and teach and guide you in this lifetime.' Tears then began to stream down my cheeks and I asked the spirit or
energy of the departed Chief: 'Are you my Spiritual Master Teacher?' And his
crisp reply was a demonstrative 'Yes!' No further words were spoken. No further questions were asked for there were none needed.

"I sat on the bench for a few more lingering moments, but it
seemed like forever. I couldn't quench my need to cry. Almost involuntarily, I rose to my feet dazed but alert. The air was quiet like it had been
before I arrived. However, when I opened the gate to leave, my body was
again welcomed by a gust of wind. And, I knew the source like I knew my
own name…Chief Red Cloud had once again evidenced his presence by
bidding me farewell.

"Hysterical tears greeted my friend as we reunited. It was hard to
stem the flow. It was hard to place into sentences the revelation I had
encountered. 'Why me?' again I asked as I have done countless times
before. Because, I reasoned, I had died as a child here—on this very same
Lakota Pine Ridge Indian Reservation which now holds the earthly
remains of Chief Red Cloud!

"I returned to New York now believing that Chief Red Cloud was
indeed my Spiritual Master Teacher who would help guide and direct my

life so that I could make proper use of my psychic gift. But doubt crept into my thinking and I craved further proof to rinse away any lingering uncertainty. So, two years later, I decided to return to South Dakota to visit my mentor's grave to bring finality to my mind. I begged to know with absolute certainty that Chief Red Cloud was my Spiritual Master Guide and if my future years were meant to be devoted to psychic healing. And, before boarding a flight to return to his resting place, I asked him to show me a sign to bring confirming affirmation.

"I did return to his gravesite with both excitement and apprehension, not knowing what to expect. But, like I always do, I felt that a message would be delivered to me by 'the positive energy of the universe.' When I barely reached the fenced-off area, I saw a pickup truck kicking up dust heading towards me, eventually coming to a halting stop. A woman first exited the vehicle and headed towards me and the resting place of Chief Red Cloud. Following behind her was a man who introduced himself as James Red Cloud, the great-great-grandson of Chief Red Cloud. Both had come to honor their progenitor.

"When I explained who I was and the purpose for my visit, a smile greeted the face of James and, with exuberant cordiality, he invited me to follow him back to the home of Chief Oliver Red Cloud, the fourth-generation direct descendent of Chief Red Cloud, who had become Chief of the Oglala Lakota, also known as the Oglala Sioux following the death of his father Charles Red Cloud. Was this the sign that I had hoped would greet me after trekking across the country on a pressing mission? Fate would not deny me an answer. So, I welcomed the invitation much like a child eager to be driven to an ice cream parlor.

"When I shared the hospitality offered by Chief Oliver Red Cloud, I learned that he was the spiritual leader of his tribe having devoted his life to preserving the rituals and heritage of his people. Living in modest quarters, an understatement, age had taken its toll and the Chief was confined to a wheelchair. Later, I was told that his age was 91.

"In the room where I was received, I noticed five pictures on the wall of Native Americans dressed in what I judged to be ceremonial attire. Instantly, my heart was drawn to one and I asked if he was Chief Red Cloud. The answer confirmed my intuition. Then, I explained my past-life regression and my visit to the Chief's gravesite two years earlier.

"'Why have you returned?' questioned Oliver. 'To satisfy my need to know if the great Chief is my Spiritual Master Guide.' Barely exhaling a breath, Chief Oliver said a simple 'Yes.' I was stunned by his rapid reply and then he assured me that he had spoken the truth. As to the matter of committing the remaining years of my life to that of a psychic-healer, he validated what I always had harbored in my thoughts—that I was meant to use my gift for a beneficent purpose.

"Not wishing to impose and to overstay my visit, I eventually excused myself and expressed gratitude that was genuinely extracted from my heart. It had taken many decades, but at last I could identify the companion who was accompanying me on my life's journey to provide insightful awareness to others—Chief Red Cloud!

"Do we all have a Spiritual Master Guide?" asked Milka excusing her interruption.

"Yes, Milka. Although you may not be privileged to know his or her name, you are also blessed with a Guardian Protector, sometimes called a 'Guardian Angel.' Know that our Guardian Protector is positive energy that surrounds our earthly being. It is that inner voice that tells us to go right not left to avoid an unseen calamity. Some call it intuition or a gut feeling, but it is a vibrating essence. While it does not make us immune from all calamities, it strives to help us lessen the dangers that are encountered as we navigate through life.

"Know further that a Spiritual Master Teacher is one who has 'touched the earth,' namely, lived at least one lifetime. A Guardian Protector, on the other hand, is an energized force that has **never** 'touched the earth,' resonating with a **higher frequency of energy**. To a skeptic, this probably sounds farfetched. But, I assure you from experience, I have firsthand knowledge that validates the bold statement I have just made.

"Often I am told by a parent that his or her child claims to have an imaginary friend who he or she talks to. I'm asked: 'Could this be a Guardian Protector?' My answer is 'most probably.' There is an innocence that young children harbor that has not yet been corrupted or compromised by worldly interactions. Captured by this purity, the energy emanating from a Guardian Protector is more easily harnessed by a child's incorruptibility.

"I've never seen the image of my Guardian Protector but I have heard her voice countless times. I asked who she was and she introduced herself to me early on and called herself 'Lucy' for short, but I believe her name may be 'Lucinda' or 'Lucia.' I've come to know that her composition is of a higher energy than my Spiritual Master Teacher and that she faithfully watches over me. She is my personal Guardian Protector.

"While my Master Teacher is not always with me, my Protector is. 'So,' you might ask, 'can I get myself into a mess even though Lucy watches over me?' Yes, indeed. Will my Protector do *her* best, or perhaps *its* best, to alter my misjudged course of action or misguided judgment? Yes, but the ultimate choice when a decision is meant to be made inevitably resides within me!

"I also know with certitude that there are other guides that engage with us, but remain unseen. You may not be aware of their presence but, as a psychic-medium, I have encountered more than a few. When I do a reading for parents when a young child has passed to *Beyond the Beyond*, a 5-year-old spirit guide named 'Lulu' helps me to connect to the infant or youngster who has transitioned from the earth. Let me highlight just one of many stories.

"Recently, I attended a barbecue in Upstate New York. There, I encountered a little girl who wore a pink frilly dress, white anklet socks, and black patent leather shoes. Her hair was curly and her temperament was impish. Once seen, she seemed to vanish from my sight; hiding I suspected. I described her to those present; however, no one identified with her and I quickly dispatched her from my memory until…destiny intervened to introduce me to her mother!

"Once I left Upstate, I attended a metaphysical life conference in Chicago. I was a guest and not a presenter. Looking for a bite to eat, I went to the hotel's restaurant. Because of the size of the conference, available seats were 'as scarce as hen's teeth' as the expression goes.

"Three ladies seated at a round table near the bar recognized my distress and graciously asked me to join them since there was a spare chair. They soon discovered that I was a psychic-medium because I mentioned that I saw a dapper black man in spirit standing by one of the ladies. When I described him, the stunned lady acknowledged that that was her deceased husband. She was, in her own words, 'blown away.'

"After sitting for awhile, one of the three ladies excused herself to puff on a cigarette in the corridor outside of the restaurant. There, fate, but more than likely Lulu, intervened. The lady who was congesting her lungs with nicotine-laced smoke met a complete stranger who introduced herself as Michelle. Striking up a conversation, the lady learned that Michelle had recently lost a daughter within the past six months. Well, you probably have guessed what happened next. Michelle was escorted to my table to see if I could connect to her lost child. Time for Lulu to step in with a message from the deceased girl!

"'Ask mommy to show you a picture of me,' Lulu's voice echoed in my brain. And I did. And then she did. And what did the little child look like? She wore a pink frilly dress, white anklet socks, and black patent leather shoes. Her hair was curly like Shirley Temple's. She was the mysterious girl that I had encountered in Upstate New York for a fleeting moment!"

"How incredible," exclaimed Milka praying that Lynn could connect to Emerson.

"If you can speak to the dead, then how do you avoid going crazy?" queried Josip. "Dead people constantly driving you nuts wanting to speak to a living loved one?"

"Josip, you ask a very good question. I was blessed with a gift to be sure, but the challenge was learning to use it wisely and to control it effectively. There is an ominous potential, as you suggest, for me to be unnerved as visitors from *Beyond the Beyond* compete to have their messages delivered to an ear residing on this earthly plane. Unless I learned to shut down the chatter, or as I like to say, 'pull down the curtain,' my brain would otherwise be assailed like the night-bombing Blitz that pounded poor London during the summer of 1940.

"Once I decided to devote myself fulltime to becoming a spiritual healer, I knew that I had to perfect my chess moves. Why? Because I was intruding upon other people's emotions. I needed to get things right much like a surgeon has to display skill lest he cause more ill than good.

"Over decades, I've attended countless spiritual developmental classes, sought out those who are renowned in the field for advice and counseling, attended lectures and workshops, and read and read and read. I am privileged to have many friends in the spiritual healing world.

"With confidence building, I began doing personal readings, slowly at first but eventually gaining momentum. As I changed lives with positive messages from the other side, my confidence and self-worth grew. I was given a gift, and I'm proud to say that I did not squander the opportunity to become an emissary channeling hope and peace to those suffering from troubling despair. As my skills blossomed from one reading to the next, abetted by research and by attending seminars and workshops, individual readings became group reading and then I was enlisted to mentor spiritual development classes throughout the United States. And now? I've garnered sufficient knowledge and wisdom worthy to share with both of you. So, to answer your original question. I've disciplined myself to 'pull down the curtain' and shut out all of the noise from *Beyond the Beyond* until I need to reach out to departed energies."

"How has being a psychic-medium changed your life?" questioned a curious mother who had lost a son weeks ago.

"Capturing but one word, I would say…'*empathy*!' I care about people like a social worker devoting his or her life trying to arrest the suffering and hopelessness of others. There is nothing on this plane of existence more traumatic than losing a loved one—a spouse, a child, a sibling, a grandparent, a special aunt or uncle, a best friend, or a person who transformed your life with a bounty of love and encouragement. Losing touch is like losing a limb. You challenge yourself to move forward and to cope with a heartbreaking loss. 'If only they weren't truly gone *forever*!' you lament with tears in your eyes. Well, the good news is that they are not gone *forever* and, thanks to my gift, I, and others, can channel their messages from *Beyond the Beyond* to provide hope and expectation."

"Expectation?" repeated Josip with a question mark attached.

"Yes, I say with abiding assurance. The expectation that one day you will surrender your bodily flesh and your true 'life force' or energy will soar to *Beyond the Beyond* to reunite with them and their enduring energy. So, to end the long version of my life story, you ask: 'How has my gift changed my life?' It has made me humble and grateful. Humble that I was blessed with a unique gift that can stitch a broken heart back together. Grateful that I can wipe away a tear and produce a lingering smile!"

Silence intruded. All conversation ceased for well over three minutes. Lynn prepared herself for the purpose of her visit…to invite one or more energies who had passed to the other side to connect with Milka and Josip from a destination defined by the psychic-medium as *Beyond the Beyond*. Would Emerson's voice be heard? Would loved ones lost in the Holocaust step forward to deliver a resonating message? Bated anticipation awaited an answer.

During the evening preceding her planned meeting with Josip and Milka, Lynn followed her traditional ritual in preparing for the reading. She guided herself to a spiritual place in her home where she lit a candle and bathed the room in soft soothing background music. Seating herself comfortably in a cushioned chair, she closed her eyes, quieted her emotions, and began a period of meditation intended to last approximately fifteen minutes. In no time, Lynn's mind transported her to an imaginary garden embroidered with the most colorful flowers of varying vibrant hues. The vision rivaled the intensity of a Renaissance artist's depiction of the Garden of Eden. Now inspired by the quietude inherent in sublime beauty, as had happened hundreds and hundreds of times before, Lynn was led to a dazzling crystal bench where she waited for her gatekeeper to usher in those with *positive* energy who were meant to join the reading the following day.

With an open and receptive mind, Lynn found herself uttering these words as she had done countless times before:

> *Father, Mother, God, Source, Universe, please protect those who I'm about to meet and surround them with your light and your love.*

Next, Lynn beseeched:

> *Ask that any message that comes from loved ones come for their highest good with ease and grace and all of the positive light.*

Following her customary practice after reciting these words, Lynn waited to see who might arrive to accompany her to her next healing reading. And, true to form, three people sat beside Lynn on that crystal bench the evening before her scheduled reading with Milka and Josip Weiss.

Before starting the reading, Lynn had an unusual request as the three sat around a small dining room table which once was shared by a cherished son.

"Josip, do you have a dictionary?"
"Lynn, yes, in my bookcase."
"Would you be kind enough to bring it to the table?"

"Why Lynn?" asked Milka confused by the request.

"It is not my request, Milka. It comes to my ears from a young voice from *Beyond the Beyond.*

With the request acknowledged by Josip, he rose from his seat and hastily retrieved a volume inspired by Noah Webster and then returned to his chair.

"Josip, kindly open the dictionary and turn the pages quickly and then randomly stop where your mind tells you to pause," instructed the psychic-medium. "I'll turn away with my back to you so that I'll not see which page you have chosen on the right or left side of the book."

With Lynn's back turned to him, Josip moistened his index finger with saliva from the tip of his tongue and began to wildly flip pages until scarcely one-fifth remained.

"Have you finished?" queried Lynn.

"Yes, finished," was Josip's puzzled retort uncertain of Lynn's intentions.

Without shifting her body or her gaze, the psychic-medium reached around to find the book with her hand. With a probing finger, guided like a laser beam, her digit stopped once it found a particular word on the left page. Was serendipity at work? Or, had the energy of a loved one about to speak orchestrated what happened next?

"Josip, what word is my finger resting on or pointing to?" questioned Lynn.

"The word is 'source'," replied Josip cradling the dictionary in his hands.

"Lynn, what does this mean?" whispered Milka with a shrunken voice.

"That we have connected to the *Source* of all understanding. Time to begin the reading. Josip, you can close the book and lay it aside. An energy is present. I feel the strong vibrational frequency of a young man with a life lesson he wishes to share."

"What is his name?" questioned Milka. "Could it be…?"

"Shush Milka!" exclaimed Josip to preempt his wife from speaking further. "Don't give clues away. If she's a true medium, then she'll supply the answer."

"Milka, Josip is right," insisted Lynn. "If this reading is to retain its integrity, don't feed me information unless I ask for clarification or verification."

"I understand. I'll still my tongue but not my excitement."

"The name of the young man has not reached me yet. Perhaps a description of him will suffice for I see his face as well as I see yours."

"Go on. Please go on," pleaded Milka anxious to know if Emerson had returned in spirit.

"Young. Not yet twenty is my educated guess. Dark brown hair. Thick and wavy. The number 3 appears. To me, it means a month. In this case, March. He's somehow connected to the month of March."

With the description of the unearthly visitor revealing itself as her son, Milka let out a muffled squeal with her hand shading her mouth to control the intensity. And then Josip put his fingers to his closed lips signaling to Milka to remain silent so as not to announce the name "Emerson."

"This boy, or rather young man, is smart. No! Smart is not generous enough. His capacity for thinking is beyond extraordinary. I see Einstein standing behind him."

"Einstein?" questioned Josip unsure of the meaning.

"Not Einstein literally. Einstein's vibrating energy surrounds him. This tells me that the young man had a brilliant mind. Does any of this make sense? Now you are free to tell me if I'm on the right track. Do you know this person?"

"Track? I'm hopping aboard the train to reunite with our son, Emerson, who was born on March 30th. The three you referred to," blurted Josip who could hardly believe his ears and constrain his exhilaration.

"Your son, the young man you call Emerson, wants to assure you that he is safe in the loving company of other family members. He said he was right! Again, he says the word 'right.'"

"Right?" repeated Milka uncertain of a meaning that required explanation.

"Yes."

Lynn hesitated for a moment to capture the full implication of the word "right" so that she could properly share it with his parents. With deep blue eyes, Lynn looked up as though she was peering into another world. Then, she refocused and stared into 2 sets of fixed eyes eager to know more.

"Milka and Josip, Emerson says he was right. He's telling me that what he calls 'consciousness' survives physical death to live on. There's more. He said that a doctor had helped him to discover that he had lived several past lives before the one with you. A doctor named Mill or Miller or....

"Emerson, be patient!" admonished Lynn speaking directly to the energy frequency that mastered her attention. "Your son is getting irritated with me for not hearing the name he has pronounced twice."

"That's my Emerson all right," declared Josip. "Impatient and impulsive."

"Now, he's telling me to ask you to fill in the blank," voiced Lynn with a degree of resignation. "Who is he referring to with the name Mill or Miller or a close variation?"

"It's Millstone. Your psychiatrist friend who recommended you to us. Dr. Milton Albert Millstone. He hypnotized Emerson and brought him back in time to previous life events in Argentina, Jordan, and Peru," declared Josip.

"So, we have validation that your son has come through. The type of validation that honors my gift of speaking with the departed," exclaimed a prideful psychic-medium who described herself as "clairvoyant, clairsentient, clairauditory"— meaning that she could see, feel, and hear those residing *Beyond the Beyond*.

"Yes, of course. But what else does Emerson have to say? Where is he? What is he doing? What is life like on the other side?" were a burst of questions advanced like the rat-a-tat of a machine gun by a father desperate to discern more.

"OK. Let's be calm and allow Emerson's energy to flow freely," voiced Lynn. "Communicating with those residing *Beyond the Beyond* is not easy. There's a lot of static interference. I have to constantly fine-tune my mind like turning the knob on a radio to hear clear voices. The departed lower their energy frequencies while I raise mine to sharpen the signal to bring clarity when the two frequencies meet. It's a delicate balancing act that has taken me years of practice to perfect."

After a momentary pause, Lynn began to laugh.

"What's so funny?" queried Josip.

"Your son is showing me...showing me...of all things, a fury sweater."

"A sweater?" questioned a confused mother.

"He's using the word 'gift,'" was Lynn's response.

"Is it cold in the place you call *Beyond the Beyond*?" quipped Josip with a sly smirk adorning his face.

"What's that Emerson?" asked Lynn as she manipulated her frequency level to understand the message that was being delivered. "He says that it pleases him to see his mother wearing it on chilly nights."

"Oh my god!" exclaimed an amazed mother. "He's talking about the vicuña sweater he brought back from Peru for me to wear."

"My head is spinning off its axis," declared Josip as he digested a message that Lynn could have never known.

Anticipation then filled the room as Lynn closed her eyes and remained silent for well over a minute. Why? Emerson began to manipulate Lynn's vocal chords and cascading sentences flowed with the intensity of a river that had surged after a heavy downpour.

"I left my body behind on the floor of my room and then discovered that I was in a place of serenity once I passed through 'Eternity's Gate.' Greeted by grandparents and aunts and uncles from both sides of the family, somehow I recognized each one even though they had long since died before I was born and was named Emerson. They told me that we had spent many past lives together and that our bond had never ever been broken. Their energy protected me and guided me when I lived as Emerson.

"After I crossed over from one reality to another, I had what was called 'a review of all of my lives.' Strangely, I remembered every single day. No, every single minute of every incarnation that I had had. And there were four. Here, the word time has no meaning. On Earth, time is nothing more than the invention of man to manage reality, which is really an illusion.

"After my review, the *Source* of all knowledge assured me that I had 'learned all of the lessons that I needed to learn,' and that there was no reason to return for a fifth life experience. In fact, there was no reason for a fourth accept to bring *joy* to my parents' lives since they had lost all of their loved ones during what is called here 'a period of despair.'

"It seems that those who have 'an incomplete spiritual life' must return to Earth again and again and again until they make themselves 'spiritually whole.' To make amends for past wrongs and to become 'pure' so that they can join 'the *oneness* of the universe' and be *one* with the *Source*.

"There is what I can best describe as a 'spiritual mountain' here, not seen but felt, which is constructed of layers of frequencies or vibrations. Once we leave Earth for good, we must try to scale to the summit to reach the highest frequency where the *Source* resides. Why? To experience the perfection of light, love, and understanding.

"How can I and others ascend upwards towards the pinnacle to achieve eternal fulfillment? It seems by inspiring those back on Earth to bring their lives in harmony with the *Source's* universal frequency. By offering guidance in ways that I'm just learning about. If those entrusted to my care make progress back on Earth, so too, I will make progress here rising to the top of the 'spiritual mountain.'

"Look for signs that I am around you. I will be guiding you. Inspiring you. By helping you, I am, at the same time, helping myself to be one with the *Source* and to achieve ultimate wisdom, which was my driving need when I lived as Emerson."

Lynn closed her eyes and, when they opened, her natural voice was returned to her. And two parents were seated in silent disbelieving awe.

Like a shriveled November leaf released from the limb of a tree to settle elsewhere, Emerson's energy or frequency detached itself from Lynn's mind. He had said what needed to be said to reassure two inconsolable parents that he had survived death to blissfully live on in some incorporeal form in a place beyond the current understanding of man.

"Ask him to return," pleaded a mother unwilling to lose touch with her departed son.

"It's not possible," began Lynn until Milka abruptly interrupted.

"There's more I need to know," came an avalanche of pleading words tumbling off of Milka's tongue.

"Someone new has come to join our conversation," declared Lynn. "There is urgency here. I can feel it. It's overwhelming energy that refuses to be denied."

"Who or what is at work?" was Josip's reciprocal expression of necessity to know.

"Please give me a moment," urged Lynn as she opened her mind to receive an incoming frequency from a new energy source.

Josip inhaled a deep breath as anticipation coursed through his body intent on reaching his brain and then his heart. After a full minute, Lynn prepared herself to be a conduit of information communicated from another spacetime dimension lying beyond the horizon of the eye of an astronomer's telescope.

"There is a man coming through," began Lynn in a slow-paced tone. "Not too young. Not too old. He has powerful muscles like a laborer working long hours in the field. What's that? Oh yes, he says that he worked in an oil refinery alongside his son. He says that he never got to see his boy fully grow up because...because...death! Horrifying, brutal death!"

The word "death" was not a shocking revelation to Josip for the person speaking was the man he had looked up to with beaming pride. It was Jakov, his father, with whom he had been employed at the same oil refinery in Osijek; that is, until his father, mother, and three sisters were arrested and, without a trial, transported in chains to a concentration camp called with distain the "Auschwitz of the Balkans." Housed with other Jews, as well as Serbs, Roma (Gypsies), and political dissidents, Josip's entire family was put to death. Then Lynn continued as Josip's chin started to quiver.

"My son was the lucky one!" the man exclaimed using Lynn's voice to carry the message. "We were all herded like cattle and sent to the slaughterhouse. Why? Because we were Jewish. Three daughters, a wife, and countless others sent to stain the earth with innocent blood. But you escaped the lion's jaws, my son. You know why?"

"That's my father Jakov!" blurted Josip. "Why father? Why me? My conscience needs to know why I alone was spared."

"Be calm, Josip," cautioned Lynn. "There is an answer. I know it is coming. I can feel it! I can sense it! Be patient."

Lynn gasped when the answer arrived. She felt an emotional surge in her heart as her lips began to move involuntarily like a marionette operated by another's *hand*.

"'Legacy-memory!' That's his two-word answer. 'To carry on the legacy and memory of your family.' And there's more. He is saying the word 'story.'"

"Story?" questioned Milka yearning to know what her father-in-law was telling them.

"He's saying: 'The story of suffering. The story of Jewish suffering. The story of Jews overcoming hardship.' His voice is now fading. It's becoming a distant echo. There is silence because another person is stepping forward with a pressing need to speak."

"Need to speak? A man or a woman?" questioned Milka hoping that it was a loved one from her lineage who had been lost at the same death camp as Josip's family.

"It's a woman with a low-pitched foreign accent. It's a weak voice coming from one who experienced many passing years. To me, she sounds Eastern European. I see an image of her last incarnation. She's a short woman with a skeleton wrapped in a thin layer of flesh. She says that: 'She has finally reunited with her husband and only child.'"

"Child?" questioned Josip.

"Yes, a son. A son who passed on early in life after being violently attacked."

"Does this woman have a name?" was Milka's anxious questioning with hope clinging to a yearning desire.

"The letter E starts her name," voiced Lynn with a straining effort to communicate to a destination she called *Beyond the Beyond*.

"My sister's name was Ezema," uttered Milka, although she knew that the description of the elderly woman did not match a sibling who had died in a concentration camp while she was still in her teens.

"No," replied Lynn asking that no information be volunteered since it might confuse the reading.

"Sorry," whined one who had lost an older sister, Ezema, and a younger brother, Micah, in the Jasenovac death camp.

"Her voice is but a whisper," sighed Lynn. "She is struggling to convey meaningful words."

Lynn paused to close her eyes tightly to try to focus her concentration and take full advantage of her unique gift of amplifying the words of those who had departed the Earth. Then, after a passing moment, what arrived was the answer to Milka's lingering inquiry.

"Elaine? No! It sounds like Lainey. No! Elena! That's it! Elena! She has a message for you both."

"And that is?" exclaimed Josip now attaching purpose to the name.

"That she once embraced the two of you and now embraces your son. She also says that you rescued her final days of life because, shortly after parting, her heart was no longer willing to beat. She says that just as you rescued her from despair and hopelessness as her time was drawing to a close, she rescued you as well and allowed your lives to take on a more important meaning."

"What important meaning?" quipped Milka leaning forward in her chair.

"To stay alive so that you could have a son. A 'specially gifted' son who she again repeats, for a second time, was 'specially gifted.' Does any of this make sense?" queried Lynn now soliciting useful information to validate the reading.

"Sense? I'm speechless! Blown away! Disbelieving at first. Lynn, you have converted a skeptic into a true believer!" cried Josip taking a deep swallow of air.

"Please explain," replied Lynn who was anxious to learn of the Weiss' connection to this woman who was straining to convey a message from a destination where death was a mere shadow of an illusion.

"Lynn," began Josip. "Elena is indeed her given name. Elena Lehmann to be complete. She speaks with a foreign Eastern European accent because she came from Bulgaria. Ruse, Bulgaria, that is. When we fled from our home city of Osijek in Croatia, we managed to steal a small boat and drift down the Drava River to escape the authorities coming to arrest us. When our boat sprang a leak, we found ourselves stranded in Ruse. After a few days on the water, we were desperately in need of a bed, a hot meal, and a warm soaking bath. Having been in a very cramped space, when our feet found the ground our legs were weak and wobbly. God led us to knock on Elena's door once we saw a *mezuzah* affixed to its frame. The symbol of our culture told us that the family inside was Jewish just like us.

"Elena welcomed us in with outstretched arms. Yes, she was elderly. Yes, she was alone having lost a husband and son years before. But, her mind was as alert as mine is today and perhaps more so. She graciously gave us the hospitality of her home for awhile. Arranged for our safe passage to Brazil and then America."

"She also gave us money," interrupted Milka. "Without her kindness, I can't imagine that we would have survived the Holocaust in Europe. Let alone have had a son...a 'specially gifted' son."

"A son who Elena now tells me has a story to be told," proclaimed Lynn with a blossoming smile adorning her face.

"What story?" asked Josip.

"A story that has a 'happy ending,'" declared Lynn using Elena's words not those of her own choosing.

"Happy ending for our son?" repeated Milka with a questioning tone manufactured by an aching heart.

"Yes, Mrs. Weiss. That death is the beginning of eternal life," exclaimed Lynn drawing upon her life's work after having conducted hundreds of spiritual readings. "'Tell your son's story' insists Elena. 'Share with others his final words intended to provide the living with comfort and hope.'"

Suddenly, an eerie silence captured the atmospherics of the room. The reading had ended and voices from *Beyond the Beyond* retreated from Lynn's mind. Josip, summoning emotions that produced cascading tears in his eyes, recast Elena Lehmann's message with those penned by Emerson when he quoted Lucius Annaeus Seneca: "The day which we fear as our last is but the birthday of eternity."

"Yes indeed, Mr. Weiss," were Lynn's confirming words. And then she formally ended the session saying:

"There is much to be learned from our short time together. First, your son, Emerson, reassured you that he is *safe* in the loving embrace of others who have surrendered their flesh to find eternal peace. Second, Josip's father chose three important words to guide your future actions... '*legacy*, *memory*, and *story*.' And finally, Elena encouraged you to tell Emerson's *life narrative* in order to walk the same path that I have chosen...to offer to others the comfort of knowing that death is not the end but merely the beginning. That we will reunite one day with loved ones to be bathed in an illuminating light of *perfected love*.

"I confess, with true honesty, that I don't have answers to how or why? I don't think that modern-day religious leaders of all persuasions, scientists, and philosophers have even begun to scratch the surface in order to reveal the unknowns about life and death. What I can tell you from a lifetime of experiences is that there is a spider web of interconnected energies residing *Beyond the Beyond* creating a **universal oneness**."

Gratitude was expressed by Milka and Josip for what had been a remarkable hour spent in the company of one who was an exceptional spiritual *hearer and healer*. Lynn received a modest sum for her work and, after Milka insisted, she agreed to return for a second time to provide healing guidance needed to deal with the loss of a young son and two entire families whose lives were extinguished in a concentration camp called Jasenovac.

FIFTY-THREE

They fought to collect their emotions and process what appeared to be beyond the pale of logic when paired with a lifetime of religious beliefs. Had voices echoed with purposeful meaning from a place where the laws of everyday reality were seemingly denied residence? Josip choked on a handful of words unable to articulate an artful message as Lynn made her way to a bustling city street polluted by traffic noise. A wave of her hand halted a taxi and she was on a mission to once again bring comfort to a grieving family.

"Josip," whispered Milka who had tears flowing endlessly down her cheeks. "I was hopeful at first and now…."

"You can't explain what clearly seems beyond explanation!" was Josip's completion of Milka's lingering unfinished sentence. "A skeptic turned believer," muttered a father who wanted to be a denier but simply couldn't propel himself to be so cavalierly dismissive.

"How do we make sense of the reading? If this was a charlatan's trick, then Lynn is the master of magic. A magician's magician."

"Making Houdini look like a foolish amateur," piped Josip, confounded by what he perceived to be a mockery of his preconditioned thoughts about death.

"But she knew nothing of us at the start. A blank piece of paper with not a hint of writing to be sure. So, to be on point. How could it be? Unless…."

"Unless it was real, Milka. Unless…'The day that we fear as our last is but the birthday of eternity,'" recalled a father once again with a rapidly beating heart as he remembered his son's last words in life that continued beyond death.

"I can't wait for our next session with Lynn," exclaimed Milka with all the anticipation of one about to read the closing chapter of a suspense novel.

Josip did not respond to his wife's last remark. His mind was excavating for an intellectual handrail to steady his reasoning. And then he involuntarily exclaimed:

"Perhaps Rabbi Oshry can make sense of this. If he can't, then I'll have to accept the unacceptable."

"That our son was right! Reincarnation is real! That the collection of our conscious memories gathered over many lifetimes somehow survive what Emerson called 'final death'! That there is an eternal universe where we are meant to eventually reunite with loved ones to create an infinite oneness!"

"'Infinite oneness,'" repeated Josip with a grin on his face. "You're beginning to sound like a budding theoretical physicist like our brilliant son."

"If Emerson didn't get his brilliance from his father, then there is only one other person who can take credit," laughed Milka with a resonance that was boastful.

The skies darkened threatening to unleash a torrent of unrelenting rain as Lynn's taxi pulled up to an address in Midtown Manhattan. She was early for her second appointment of the day and she used the opportunity to duck into a coffee shop to process her feelings and to calm her nerves. Seated with a hot cup of herbal tea to keep her company, she closed her eyes as her head drifted upwards. Although she was not privy to the reason which prompted her next reading, like the storm clouds gathering overhead, Lynn sensed a foreboding warning. Suddenly, goose bumps running down her arms and legs signaled that her intuition was trustworthy. And, she let out an involuntary sigh.

The hot tea instructed the goose bumps to wither away but still Lynn's apprehension persisted. Out of the corner of her right eye, she spotted the silhouette of a young man but, once she blinked her eyes, he was gone. "Emerson," Lynn silently whispered to herself. "His energy has followed me here and I need to banish him back to *Beyond the Beyond* or I'll never have success with my next reading." Her admonishment worked for she could feel his frequency fade like a startled bird taking fleeting flight.

Looking at her watch, Lynn realized that fifteen minutes had evaporated and that she needed to knock on the door of Rene and Steven
Demerest. Not privy to the urgency that attached itself to Rene's call to
make an appointment, Lynn instinctively knew that this reading could not
be delayed, so she shuffled her schedule to accommodate a new client.

Received at the door of a modest apartment which spoke of unpre-
tentiousness, Lynn was welcomed by a couple in their early twenties. In
silent contemplation, two words entered the psychic-medium's mind
woven together—birth-death.

By the time the 30-minute reading concluded, Lynn had connected
with Gailene who had passed through Eternity's Gate three weeks before.
It was a stillbirth occurring during delivery. The doctor's explanation,
laced with sympathy, suggested an unfortunate problem with the placenta.

Needless to say, Rene and Steven were devastated by the loss of
their first child. According to a tearful expectant mother: "It ruptured nine
months of hopes and dreams." And thus, a nursery, adored with pink-
painted walls and wishful expectations, found itself vacant and deficient of
purpose.

"Why did she die without opening her eyes?" asked a quivering
Rene.

After capturing Gailene's frequency and blending it with her own,
Lynn replied using the infant's manifested thoughts:

"The *Source* called me home to fulfill another destiny."
"What destiny?" questioned a mournful father.
"I can't be sure," replied Lynn who then continued. "Be comforted
in knowing that Gailene is in the embrace of eternal peace and love.
What's that?" Lynn strained to keep her frequency paired to Gailene's.
"Your daughter has an uplifting message for you."
"Uplifting?" questioned Rene evincing confusion.
"That soon a healthy son will be delivered to your waiting arms and
that Gailene will always be there to protect and guide him throughout his
life."

While the threatening storm clouds produced no rain outside to wet
a cheek, inside the Demerest home experienced a contrary outcome as

Rene, Steven, and Lynn wiped away an ocean of tears accompanying parting goodbyes.

Stripped of her mental and emotional vitality after two very difficult heart-tugging readings, Lynn boarded a train for a return trip home. Once she walked through the threshold, she was embraced by her husband, Dennis, and, one by one, her four children who were eager to learn of the events of the day. The normal chatter around the dinner table that evening, however, was quieted once everyone read the exhaustion on Lynn's face. It was an all too familiar scenario. Mom's healing work had left her physically drained and what she required besides a hot bath and restful sleep was calming stillness to allow her mind's frequencies to become reinvigorated.

It had been a stressful day indeed, but, in this instance, more intense given the tragic stories that unfolded. Like other readings, the passing days would cloud Lynn's memory as new strangers reached out to her to eliminate throbbing anguish in order to substitute solace. For a lingering moment, though, Emerson and Gailene clung to her psyche stubbornly refusing to let go.

As the clock on the nightstand approached 10:30 PM, Lynn rested her head on her pillow seeking to sedate the stress brought about by her calling. With Dennis fast asleep by her side, Lynn yearned to join him in a state of REM slumber. But, there was an intruder in the room intent on keeping her up. It was the silhouette of the young man who had materialized in the coffee shop. It was a vibrational frequency that identified itself as "Emerson."

After years of mastering her gift of communicating with the departed, Lynn had learned, in her words, "to pull down the curtain" to keep out uninvited energies. She needed to preserve her private space to maintain her sanity lest she be bombarded by voices constantly emanating from *Beyond the Beyond*. Perfecting the skill, Lynn became most adept at keeping Eternity's Gate bolted when necessity dictated. But now, somehow the lock had been stealthy picked by a young man with a clever metaphoric *hand*.

"Curtain closed! Curtain closed!" Lynn muttered to herself as her face dug deeper into her pillow. But her desires were being thwarted by a potent energy that she had misjudged earlier in the day. Lynn now realized that Emerson's "frequency" had been greatly amplified once he passed through Eternity's Gate and took up residence *Beyond the Beyond*. And Lynn whispered to herself: "He's going to be a force to be reckoned with!"

Lynn knew that she could only get rid of her unwelcomed guest by tuning into his desires. So, she aligned her psychic frequencies to his and gained the reason for his haunting stalking. Once she did, and she expressed her agreement, Emerson returned from whence he had come. And his message delivered with mysterious undertones?

"I am preparing to change my parents' lives forever and I need your help to assist me with my plan!"

Lynn would have a restless sleepless night because the entity named "Emerson" had manifested an energy that she had never encountered before!

FIFTY-FOUR

66 "T ime"...the word crept into his mind like the lyrics of a song refusing to leave as Josip prepared to close his haberdashery shop on the Lower Eastside of Manhattan. Perhaps it was the clock on the wall that had triggered the arrival of the word. After all, it was six in the evening and the last customer had long since departed with a smile and a purchase. No, "time" was whispered into his ear by another to be received by his subconscious mind and then quickly transported to his conscious awareness. "Time" repeated Josip attaching it to his age...46; then the year...1965; then the month...11; then the weeks since Emerson had died...7; and then the days since Lynn had performed a life changing reading...3.

After dimming the lights in the store to signal to the general public that the business night had ended, Josip paused for a moment before he prepared to walk several blocks to reach his tenement apartment and a waiting Milka.

Sitting on a stool positioned behind a cash register, Josip wondered about the word "time" and then recalled Emerson's valedictorian high school speech to the graduating class of 1964. In it, a proud father attentively listened to his son make a bold declaration that suddenly returned complete to Josip's recollection as though Emerson were reciting it again to him so that he could contemplate the message to gain a deeper understanding of life:

> *Time and space are an illusion manufactured by the human mind to try to understand reality. Antiphon the Sophist, in the 5th century BCE, wrote that "Time is not a reality, but a concept or a measure."*

> *In 1781, Immanuel Kant insisted: "We must rid ourselves of the notion that space and time are actual qualities in things themselves... all bodies, together with the space in which they are, must be considered nothing but mere representations in us, and*

exist nowhere but in our thoughts…It is our mind that processes information about the world and gives it order…our mind supplies the conditions of space and time to experience objects."

Then Josip recalled Lynn's reading and the words spoken through her by his son.

Here, the word time has no meaning. On Earth, time is nothing more than the invention of man to manage reality, which is really an illusion.

"Time" reiterated Josip trying to shake it loose from his brain. And with the passage of a minute, it took flight.

Josip lifted himself from the stool…walked to the door where he reversed a sign that said "open" so that it would read "closed"…locked the door with his key…and pointed his feet in the direction of home. "What is life and death really about?" queried Josip. "Perhaps Rabbi Oshry might have insight into the answer!" was his finishing thought since he and Milka had an appointment to meet with the rabbi on Sunday.

Rabbi Ephraim Oshry sat in his study at the Beth Hamedrash Hagodol Synagogue as morning faded. He awaited a grief counseling session with Milka and Josip Weiss that was meant to bring consolation to the lives of two grieving parents.

An Orthodox rabbi born in 1914, Ephraim Oshry was one of just a handful of rabbis who managed to survive the Holocaust. Born in Kupiškis, Lithuania, in 1941, as the tentacles of the Nazi war effort gobbled up country after country and strangled countless communities,

Ephraim's family and others were forced into the Kovno Ghetto, a ghetto established by Nazi Germany to hold Lithuanian Jews living in Kaunas, the second-largest city in Lithuania. It was a time of collaboration when Hitler's forces, aided and abetted by Lithuanian sympathizers, abandoned their consciences and ruthlessly sought to exterminate all Jews.

Recounting the Holocaust experience in a book titled *The Annihilation of Lithuanian Jewry*, Rabbi Oshry described the deprivation that followed the Nazi invasion. "Despite being starved and beaten, the Jews continued to study Torah in secret and risked their lives in order to fulfill the *mitzvah* (God's commandments)."

While confined in what became a concentration camp, Oshry penned his "responsa" trying to make sense of the events of the Holocaust. In it, he addressed his feelings about "human nature, God, and Jewish ethics." To preserve his writings, he buried them in the ground and, when the war ended, he retrieved them. In 1959, he published his reflections under the title *She'eilos Uteshuvos Mima'amakim* ("Questions and Responses from the Depths").

When liberated in August 1944, Ephraim and his wife Frieda Greenzwieg, who had miraculously survived the atrocities committed at Auschwitz, traveled to Rome where the rabbi founded a yeshiva for refugee children. Six years later, he relocated to Montreal, Canada, with his family and a number of yeshiva students. Two years thereafter, in 1952, he moved to New York City accepting the position of rabbi at the Beth Hamedrash Hagodol Synagogue.

A respectful knock on his closed door propelled Rabbi Oshry to his feet. With haste, he welcomed Josip and Milka Weiss into his private office and motioned each to take a seat in a chair positioned in front of his desk.

"This is a trying time for you both, I know," came the rabbi's sympathizing words. "So young to be gone with such a promising future lying ahead of him. A theoretical physicist studying at Stanford. And now, only a fleeting memory of what was and a faded promise of what might have been."

"Rabbi, we have many questions to draw upon your years of acquired wisdom," began Josip in a subdued tone. "The coroner's report recorded the cause of Emerson's death as 'Unknown.' How can a boy simply vanish like a puff of smoke that wasn't ignited by fire?" asked Milka.

"God acts in mysterious ways for mysterious reasons," was the rabbi's curt reply deprived of any hint of compassion.

"Rabbi, what does our Torah tell us about the afterlife?" queried Josip concealing the true reason for the question—the recent reading with Lynn with perhaps another to follow.

"Well Josip, to be perfectly frank, the Torah does not speak of an afterlife in any detail. This has led many rabbinic scholars to speculate about what happens after we die. The Torah is more concerned about living rather than dying. What in Hebrew we call *Olam Ha Zeh*, meaning 'This World.' The intention is to devote ourselves to living a good life here and now.

"As for the future, we speak of *Olam Ha Ba*, or translated 'The world to come.' It is existence at the end-of-days after the Messiah has come and God has sat in judgment of both the living and the dead."

"What about reincarnation?" questioned Milka.

"It is not part of our religious beliefs," quipped the rabbi.

"Rabbi, we have met someone who has helped us connect to those who have departed. We have heard the words of our son, my father, and a friend who helped us escape the Holocaust," were words delicately expressed by Josip which were designed to avoid offending the rabbi and the teachings of the Torah.

"If it is true, then the person has a true gift from God. If it is false, then God's punishment will be harsh when He sits in judgment at the end-of-days. I'll withhold my opinion for now and merely say that if this brings you comfort as you grieve the loss of your son, then so be it."

"It does bring us some comfort," exclaimed Milka. "But Rabbi, it does not release us from the day-to-day suffering we are forced to endure when we pass by Emerson's empty bedroom."

"Mr. and Mrs. Weiss, try to find comfort by studying the Torah, faithfully attending services, and praying each day to God. Know that we at Beth Hamedrash Hagodol Synagogue are one family, your extended family," counseled the rabbi.

"Yes, *ONE!*" proclaimed Josip remembering his son's reference to being "*one* with the *Source*."

"When I am called upon to do a eulogy for a departed soul, I oft-times quote from a poem written by John Donne, an English poet and cleric. I have *done* it, pardon the pun, so many times that the words cling to my memory and to my tongue. Let me recite it for you.

> *No man is an island,*
> *Entire of itself,*
> *Every man is a piece of the continent,*
> *A part of the main.*
> *If a clod be washed away by the sea,*
> *Europe is the less.*
> *As well as if a promontory were*
> *As well as if a manor of thy friend's*
> *Or of thine own were:*
> *Any man's death diminishes me,*
> *Because I am involved in mankind,*
> *And therefore never send to know for whom the bell tolls;*
> *It tolls for thee.*

"The poet reminds us that humanity is one family. Our life forces are all interconnected. The loss of one person, known or unknown to us, affects our lives whether we recognize it or not. So, the departure of your son, Emerson, is a loss that touches all of our hearts and diminishes us all in some unseen way.

"How can you deal with grief? They say that there are five stages that you need to go through. Let me briefly mention them.

Denial..........Not willing to accept the loss.

Anger..........When denial proves futile and one's emotions become elevated. People often respond by saying—"It's not fair."; "How could this have happened?"

Bargaining...As people are want to say—"If only he'd come back to life, things would be different;" or "I'd give anything to have him back."

Depression....Often expressed—"I miss my loved one, why go on?"

Acceptance...We understand that dying is part of the cycle of life.

"Milka and Josip, work through these stages of grieving giving consoling reassurance to each other along the way. In time, acceptance will rule your lives and you will cease shedding tears allowing you to move forward with your lives. Know that your rabbi and your fellow congregants are here to give you encouraging support. It is our faith and our Covenant with God that allows us to carry on in troubling times. It inspired me to survive the Holocaust and to live a righteous life. It will have the same healing power for you."

Milka and Josip expressed gratitude for the rabbi's understanding kindness. But, they wondered whether Lynn Van Praagh-Gratton could fill in the blanks that the rabbi had left behind when he freely admitted that: "The Torah does not speak of an afterlife in any detail."

FIFTY-FIVE

The fall weather had turned decidedly chillier as Thanksgiving 1965 was about to be celebrated in a sprinkling of days. For the Weiss family of two, it would not be a day to offer thanks. But, for another family residing a few blocks away, it would be a welcomed opportunity to occupy five chairs and share dinner, stories, and love.

Jerome and Edith Katzman had much to be grateful for. He, a talented real estate attorney, and she a housewife raising three precocious children—Sarah, age 18, attending Columbia University in the city with an anticipated major in Classical Literature; Brian, age 15, likely to draw the attention of several Ivy League colleges based upon his academic credentials and his prowess on the athletic field; and finally, Kate, age 8, who Edith affectionately called "the runt of the litter," arriving in Edith's belly as a complete surprise when she had thought that her infant rearing days had finally ended for good.

Although the Katzman family belonged to the Beth Hamedrash Hagodol Synagogue, they never made the acquaintance of Josip and Milka Weiss and were not aware that they had lost a son. The reason resided in the fact that the congregation consisted of a great number of families and, more to the point, Jerome Katzman evinced just a passing interest in his faith, attending services only when the High Holy Days arrived or when an elbow in his side from Edith persuaded him to make peace with God.

Edith and Jerome had taken a deep breath when it came time for Sarah to choose a university to attend. She was a straight "A" student with a probing mind who attracted offers that extended from New York to California. When Columbia offered Sarah a full scholarship which included tuition, books, and a dormitory room, the Katzmans jumped at the opportunity. To save money? No! A more seductive reason—to have their daughter living closer to home.

Of the three children, Sarah had a way of wrapping her emotions around your heart. She was born with an innocence that spoke of celestial purity. "Naïve" was a word that early on affixed itself to a description of Sarah. In time, however, that word would fade to be replaced by "virtuous." There was a selfish reason why Jerome and Edith had yearned to have their eldest child attend a college just a local train ride from home—to watch over her as doting parents often aspire to do.

Sarah had begun her studies three months earlier spending most of her time in the university's prestigious library. Invited to join a sorority and to fraternize with boys on weekends, Sarah demurred and offered as an excuse both the rigors of her area of study and her ambition to become a Rhodes Scholar. Her goal in life had not yet coalesced in her mind, but she hoped to earn a PhD from either Cambridge or Oxford and then? Well, there was plenty of time to define the word "then."

While Sarah didn't fuss much with clothes or makeup, she spoiled the eyes of young men with the temptation of coyness. Five-foot-two, with long black flowing hair tied into a ponytail, her dazzling dark brown eyes invited more than a glance, but less than a stare. There was just something about Sarah that made you want to learn her name and to share a story or a laugh.

As Emerson Weiss discovered as he searched for the entry to Eternity's Gate, life is as unpredictable as the path taken by a fast-moving tornado. And it would be no different for Sarah Beth Katzman, for little did the college freshman know that fate would entangle her in a web from which she would have trouble escaping. Little did she know that destiny would align her horoscope with the amazing talents of Lynn Van Praagh-Gratton!

Milka Weiss was having strange dreams and finding coins in the oddest places. In 1936, the song "Pennies from Heaven" previewed in a movie by the same name; however, Milka was not finding pennies but Winged Liberty Head dimes. There was one that took refuge by her night table. One found in a supermarket isle in plain sight for anyone to retrieve. One lying at her feet when she noticed a shiny object as she prepared to cross a busy Manhattan street. And even one begging to be picked up from her front doormat. Hoping that it was a sign from Emerson, she put them in a small cloth pouch and slept with it once she tucked it securely under her pillow. Josip used a Yiddish word to describe his wife's behavior—

meshuga, translated as "nonsense, craziness, or silliness." But, Milka swiped away the word like she was employing a swatter to dispense with an annoying insect, duly pointing out to Josip that each coin had a "wing, perhaps an angel's wing."

Then there was a recurring dream that stuck in her mind when she awoke in the morning, and she wondered whether the coins were sending a message through her pillow to her psyche. They always started with a doorbell ring. When Milka went to welcome the caller and looked through the peephole, she repeatedly saw a young child, perhaps six or seven, who begged to be let in. The innocent appearing girl said that she didn't have a daddy and that her mommy didn't want her anymore. When Milka asked her name, with tears cascading down her pale cheeks, she replied: "Emily." Each dream ended in the same fashion. Emily was seated at the Weiss' dinner table with a smile adorning her face, an elated beaming smile shared by Milka and Josip.

A mother who had just lost her son wondered if Emily was an imaginary child sent by Emerson to bring comfort to her resting and waking mind. And a coincidence was not lost on Milka. Both names started with "Em." In Milka's heart, there was only one person who could make sense of the strange events coloring her life— Lynn Van Praagh-Gratton! But holidays and Lynn's growing schedule would have to postpone a second visit to well after the start of the New Year.

Lynn's reputation had taken a giant leap forward after her reading with Josip and Milka Weiss. It accelerated like a diver launching herself from an Olympic springboard with her arms stretched spread eagle as she flew through the air. A featured article in the *New York World-Telegram and Sun* followed by a profile in *Life* magazine catapulted Lynn into the public limelight. The psychic-medium was propelled by necessity to hire a personal secretary to take calls and manage her congested appointment book. Celebrities requested private readings, as did politicians and business entrepreneurs. Lynn invariably had a suitcase packed and ready to fly from one city to another to communicate messages from *Beyond the Beyond* to waiting ears craving and, at times, begging for answers.

Private readings competed with group readings, and Lynn regretted taking time away from her husband and her children. But, she soothed her conscience by reminding herself that she had been entrusted with a unique gift of *hearing and healing* that was meant to ease pain and to implant a message of hope in countless aching hearts.

Circumstances now dictated that Lynn handpick her clients since demand for her services was growing beyond the hours that consumed her normal working day. Old clients, by necessity, would have to be replaced with new clients with one conspicuous exception—Milka and Josip Weiss! Why? Because there was a vibrational energy entangled with her own that refused to disengage. He was scheming from *Beyond the Beyond* and had made his intentions demonstratively known. And Lynn, as hard as she tried, could not release Emerson's words from her conscious memory...

> *"I am preparing to change my parents' lives forever*
> *and I need your help to assist me with my plan!"*

FIFTY-SIX

A s revelers, deprived of elbow room, stood shivering in New York City's Time Square to usher in 1966, the mood of the crowd lacked the usual spirited enthusiasm. Instead, it was fed by an undercurrent of emotions that were sober and subdued. The Vietnam War, also called the Second Indochina War or, according to the North Vietnamese, the Resistance War Against America, was accelerating with explosive intensity. Less than a year earlier, on March 8, 1965, 3,500 U.S. Marines were deployed to South Vietnam signaling the beginning of a ground war. By December, nine months later, President Lyndon B. Johnson had authorized the troop strength to grow exponentially to nearly 200,000. Meaning? Wooden caskets would be flown home for military burials while hearts of loved ones shriveled in their chests!

U.S. Army General William Childs Westmoreland, who commanded American forces in Vietnam starting in 1964, predicted a swift victory "by the end of 1967." He would be proved wrong on two accounts. First, the United States military would not be victorious but would suffer an ignominious defeat, vanquished by a wily enemy who implemented a strategy which came to be known as "guerilla warfare." Second, direct U.S. military involvement persisted well past 1967 until it finally ended in August 1973. And the blood spilled for a senseless war that achieved nothing in the jockeying for position to gain regional supremacy? 58,315 Americans dead; 303,644 men and women wounded!

When the clock struck twelve midnight at the Weiss apartment to dispense with 1965, no one was up to take notice or to exchange a hug or a well-placed kiss. Milka and Josip had little to celebrate because three had forlornly become two. Had their son been alive, Milka wondered whether he would have been yanked out of school and sent to fight an ugly meaningless war. This moment in history did not mirror the time when she and Josip fled Europe to elude capture by Nazi and Fascist armies. This new "advertised enemy" was not marching to the drumbeat of "world domination." This new "advertised enemy" had not vowed to wipe out a race of people!

Milka grieved as she saw coffin after coffin returned home draped in an American flag. She saw tears flow from the eyes of mothers just like the tears that knew no ending when she laid Emerson to rest.

As the first sprigs of sunlight peered through her bedroom window days after 1966 took charge, Milka opened her eyes before her husband awakened. Not to disturb him, she stilled her muscles and peered at the ceiling allowing her mind to drift. "How can I help those who are now, and soon will be, grieving mothers?" she challenged her reason. "By volunteering" came a heartfelt reply generated by a whisper germinating from *Beyond the Beyond*!

Life had grown stagnant and stale for Milka Weiss now that her husband was engaged six days a week running his busy haberdashery shop and an empty bedroom served as a diurnal reminder that what was once could no longer be. She yearned to fill the hollow emptiness that left her psyche want of purpose, so, with the support of Josip, she placed a call to the local chapter of the American National Red Cross to ask if they could use a helping hand.

A humanitarian organization founded by Clarissa "Clara" Harlowe Barton on May 21, 1881, the Red Cross became proactive in providing emergency assistance, disaster relief, and educational services. During the Vietnam War, it stepped forward to offer emergency and non-emergency services to U.S. military personnel and their families sending care packages abroad to the troops, communicating messages from loved ones to soldiers in the field, comforting family members when bad news arrived from the war zone, and more, much more!

When Milka contacted the Red Cross chapter having its office in Midtown Manhattan to volunteer her two hands and her righteous heart, they were only too pleased to have her join their ranks. By the third week in January, after only two weeks on the job, she made a most favorable impression on Kathleen Wrenger, the Chief Executive Officer of the chapter, by arriving early, staying late, and by her willingness to take on menial as well as consequential work. As days progressed, Milka's dedication was becoming contagious in the office and, for the first time, she began to make peace with the loss of her son as she experienced the tragic hardships borne by others when notified of the death of a loved one.

For Milka, a troubling day was swiftly approaching on her horizon, menacing like an arrow aimed straight at her heart. March 30th was bearing down on her like a freight train that had lost its brakes—it was the calendar day when Emerson was meant to celebrate his 19th birthday.

Milka had hoped that Lynn might be available for a promised second reading on her son's special day. A bereft mother wanted desperately to communicate a message of love to her boy, but, unfortunately, the psychic-medium's schedule, planned well in advance, had her in Denver, Colorado, for an appearance on a local television talk show, and, the following day, standing before a sold out audience in a large auditorium setting.

"How can I honor the memory of Emerson on the last Wednesday in March?" questioned Milka, silently challenging herself. And then the answer was delivered not by Lynn Van Praagh-Gratton but by another reliable source—war footage from Vietnam.

It was a critical time when blood donations were straining the nation's reserves. After addressing the local chapter's Board of Directors, Milka asked if she could coordinate a blood drive on her son's birthday. In preparation for the presentation, Milka prepared a detailed outline that sought to enlist the support of New York City's colleges and universities to sponsor blood drives on their respective campuses. Reading from her notes, she rattled off the names:

New York University
Columbia University
Fordham University
St. John's University
City College of New York
Pace University
Hunter College
The New School for Social Research
Cooper Union
Yeshiva University

Milka's bold proposed undertaking was received with enthusiastic approbation. And, she was put in charge of coordinating the single-day event, a day to honor her son and those who put themselves in harm's way for country, forsaking personal desires.

Getting right to work, Milka assigned a Red Cross staff member to the ten institutions. Each staff member was charged with the task of securing the cooperation of the university's or college's administration, selecting a student to serve as a liaison to help to coordinate all details, undertaking a public relations campaign on campus, and recruiting medical volunteers to assist in the collection and preservation of donated blood. For herself, Milka chose Columbia University. And the person who volunteered to be her on-campus contact? A college freshman named Sarah Beth Katzman.

Lynn Van Praagh-Gratton had oft-times tutored in her various group and individual readings that: "There are no *coincidences* in life." And the pairing of Milka with Sarah? Lynn's intuitive answer would have been, if asked the question—"A *hand* outstretched from *Beyond the Beyond!*"

Not to be left out of the patriotic fervor expressed and embraced by his wife, Josip did his part to support the men and women dressed in military attire. He invited the general public to his men's clothing store on the 30th of March and advertised that all, yes ALL, proceeds of the day would be donated to the Red Cross to compliment the blood drives being held on campuses throughout the city.

Assisting a new customer who had entered his shop, Josip offered advice concerning an appropriate tie that flattered the blue pin-striped suit the man was wearing. When Josip asked the patron his name, the well-groomed gentleman said "Jerome Katzman." The name did not ring a bell in Josip's ear; but, it would have in Milka's since he was the father of Sarah who, that very day, was working alongside her at the Columbia University blood drive. Was this a fortuitous happenstance? Lynn Van Praagh-Gratton's reply would have been: "There are no *coincidences* in life," leaving one to wonder whether a *hand* had orchestrated the introduction of Josip to Jerome from a place called *Beyond the Beyond*.

FIFTY-SEVEN

Lynn Van Praagh-Gratton finally arrived home after a grueling six days on the road. It was good to reconnect with Dennis and the children and to once again attend to long neglected household tasks. It was a time of renewal. Spring flowers were beginning to serenade the senses and the chill of winter hastily retreated suspending its return for at least another seven months.

Once she reviewed her schedule with her personal secretary, Lynn saw that Milka and Josip had expressed a pressing need for a second reading. This did not surprise Lynn because the energy of their son had intruded uninvited on several occasions during her visit to Colorado. As hard as she tried to suppress his vibrational frequency, he persisted and persisted and persisted and managed to peek through her closed mental curtain which was intended to keep uninvited intruders out.

Lynn knew that Emerson was using his metaphysical *hand* to manipulate actions back on planet Earth, more particularly, in New York City. What maneuvering scheme he had up his metaphoric sleeve, however, was not yet clear to the psychic-medium; but, she knew with an undeterred confidence that he was busily plotting and planning as he once confided to her— "to change my parents' lives forever." Little did Lynn realize that his machinations involved Milka's seemingly chance encounter with Sarah as well as Josip's seemingly chance encounter with Sarah's father!

On Sunday evening, April 24, 1966, Lynn Van Praagh-Gratton broke with tradition and scheduled a reading for Milka and Josip Weiss at their apartment at 7:00 PM. Ordinarily, Lynn would have reserved the evening to spend a relaxing night with her husband, Dennis. But, circumstances strangled that tradition.

The English-language proverb with an unknown author counsels: "Necessity is the mother of invention." And, as the wisdom related to Lynn's life, it dictated that she had to juggle her personal life demands in order to satisfy the growing needs and expectations of others.

Lynn's reception at the Weiss home was acknowledged with a hug from Josip and a kiss on the right cheek from Milka. Seated at the dining room table as they had done one time before, the three engaged in a give-and-take discourse.

"Lynn, we can't thank you enough for fitting us into your very busy schedule, especially on a Sunday," was Milka's heartfelt expressed appreciation laced with an implied apology.

"My life has certainly been a whirlwind lately," confided the psychic-medium. "Frankly, I can't keep up with the demand on my time. Honestly, I probably wouldn't be sitting with you this evening if it weren't for your son who's driving me crazy."

"Crazy?" repeated Josip with a question mark punctuating the word.

"He's up to something all right. Your brilliant son that is. He intruded into the privacy of my bedroom after our first reading to deliver a message. I spied his silhouette in the corner of the room and his energy frequency captured mine like a fisherman retrieving a fish on a hook with a hand-held net."

"Lynn, what was his message?" asked Milka with a palpitating pulse anxious to know.

"Milka, brace yourself. He said that he planned on changing your life and Josip's life forever!"

"How?" questioned Josip with the flavor of alarm souring his tone.

"He hasn't shared his plans with me yet," admitted the psychic-medium. "But, he assured me that somehow I would be drawn into his master plan."

"Is this good news or bad?" queried Milka suddenly experiencing trepidation.

"Probably good for both of you. But for others penciled into the equation? Who knows? Let me pause to ask you both a question."

"Shoot," insisted Josip.

"Have you experienced anything unusual in your life that might hint that Emerson is around you or communicating with either of you?"

"Strange that you should ask that question," blurted Milka.

"Yes? Please detail what's going on."

"Well Lynn, two things have played with my sanity," began Milka. "First, dimes! I've found a number in the oddest places. Second, a reoccurring dream with the same little girl coming to visit time and time again. A little girl named Emily."

"Tell me about the coins and the dreams."

"Lynn, not pennies, or nickels, or quarters. Just dimes. By my bed. In the supermarket. At my feet as I crossed a street. Even on our welcome mat to greet me when I came home one day. As for the dreams. A little girl named Emily who has been abandoned and now asks us to take her in and look after her. She is a sweet and precious child about 6 to 8 years old."

"And did you take her in?"

"Yes, Lynn. And she brought us joy in a way that our Emerson had blessed our lives."

"Josip, anything strange or unusual that you've noticed?" questioned Lynn.

"Not really. Nothing that I can point a finger at."

Had Milka and Josip shared experiences and been privy to the actions of a puppeteer residing *Beyond the Beyond*, they might have brought up the names Jerome and his daughter, Sarah, Katzman. But neither Josip, who met Jerome, nor Milka, who worked with Sarah, shared his or her encounter to weave the two people together.

"To explain the dimes and dreams, let me say this from years of experience," began the psychic-medium. "Dimes are not inadvertently lost from a purse or dropped from a hole in a pocket. They are deposited by energies wanting to let loved ones know that they are around them. I have no doubt that Emerson is the culprit in this instance. OK. Your son just entered my mind and my inner vision sees him nodding his head and laughing. Hysterically laughing.

"The dreams are yet another way for energies to engage with us and to send messages. My advice, write down your dreams and see if a pattern emerges as it relates to your day-to-day life. Also, spend time in a quiet spot in the house, close your eyes, still your nerves, dismiss all thoughts from your head and meditate. Let your mind drift and wander on its own. See if you can pick up any energies or merge with other frequencies. See if a picture forms in your mind or a voice whispers words into your ears. Try to be '*one*' with the *Source*. You may be surprised at the messages you will receive."

"Messages from Emerson?" speculated Josip aloud.

"Perhaps from Emerson or another family member communicating from *Beyond the Beyond*."

"What does Emerson have to say about this little girl named Emily? The child I dream about frequently?" asked Milka craving to know the meaning surrounding the constant visitations.

"I'll try to channel Emerson," remarked Lynn. "Strangely for a young man with much to say, he's silent. As silent as a criminal taken into custody and invoking his 5th Amendment rights. What this? Your son is laughing again. He's plotting something for sure. But plotting what? 'Wait and see,' is his three-word answer. And now his frequency is gone. Vanished. He has severed the connection between us. What a character your son is."

"Wily like a pickpocket who just stole your wallet when you looked at your watch when he asked for the time," chuckled Josip.

"This is what I'd like you both to do between now and our next meeting sometime in the future."

"Tell us Lynn," insisted Milka.

"Keep your psychic eyes and ears open. Allow your mind to ask questions to those energies occupying the place I call *Beyond the Beyond*. The more you ask, the more you will receive. Meditate! Pray! And keep notes of dreams or odd happenings that don't come along with an easy explanation. Compare your observations with each other. Know that we all are blessed with psychic gifts, but we each have to master the art of using them. The more you try to open up to the *Source* of 'light and love and understanding,' the more you will realize that messages will be waiting for you in your psychic mailbox.

"Well, my time with you must end and I must be on my way. Today, this meeting has no fee attached. Consider it a gift, not from me but from your son."

"But...." began Josip as he was about to reach into his pocket.

"No buts," insisted Lynn as she rose from the table to head for the door. "Emerson is a remarkable energy with a frequency that I have rarely encountered. I have come to realize that he has two driving ambitions now that he has left this earthly plane. First, to strive to bring meaning to your lives to fill the void of emptiness once he departed for Eternity's Gate."

"And two?" questioned Milka.

"To become one with the *Source*— the eternal depository of spiritual knowledge and everlasting love nurtured by the purity of radiant light!"

FIFTY-EIGHT

J une arrived just in time for Dennis to take advantage of vacation time to briefly separate from work while four children prepared for their summer break from school to romp and play. For her part, Lynn decided to dispense with readings for several weeks to clear her mind and to become a full-time wife and mother. Many sunny days were penciled into the calendar to be spent at Coney Island, a peninsular residential neighborhood in the southwestern portion of the borough of Brooklyn which was a destination for families to stroll on the boardwalk, stop for a bite to eat, especially a Nathan's hot dog with fries, visit the amusement park, or just soak up the sun on the beach and cool off in the refreshing water.

"No readings whatsoever for the next three weeks," was Lynn's instruction to her personal secretary. "Not even one! My curtain has now been lowered tightly shut and no visitors from *Beyond the Beyond* are welcomed. I don't care if the President of the United States calls. Tell him to try again in July!" was Lynn's swift reprimanding tone to the woman who methodically logged the medium's appointments.

Halfway into the month that squeezed itself between May and July came a call on Lynn's private phone at home, a telephone that was intended to receive calls from only relatives and friends. For business calls, another line had been installed to build a bridge intended to separate work from a personal life. But just past 8:00 PM on a Wednesday evening, Lynn's private phone rang and the caller was neither a relative nor a friend!

"How did you get this number?" questioned Lynn to an unnamed male caller who sought to book a reading for his employer.

"When you work for one of the wealthiest men in the world, anything is possible," came the blunt reply from a man with a deep-throated voice who would later introduce himself simply as John.

"What's this about?" asked Lynn quizzically.

"My boss desires a reading for himself and his wife," arrived a curt reply.

"Why?"

"You're a famous psychic-medium. You tell me," was the stranger's smug retort.

"To connect to a lost loved one, I suppose."

"Your antenna is up and working well," laughed John.

"But I'm off for the next several weeks. No readings. Absolutely none. I promised myself and my family."

"Make one important exception!" insisted the mysterious caller. "Kindly know that my employer doesn't abide taking 'no' for an answer. Anyway, he will make it worth your while to visit his estate in the Hamptons on Long Island."

"Worth my while?"

"Yes, Mrs. Van."

"That's Van Praagh-Gratton."

"Whatever. For your time, he's authorized me to tell you that he will pay $500 in hard cold cash."

Hearing that number caused Lynn to gasp. It was more than twenty times her 1966 fee. Sounding like a mafia boss, the voice on Lynn's private phone admonished: "This is an offer you can't refuse."

Lynn hesitated for a fraction of a moment intrigued by the offer and curious about the man who was willing to pay an exorbitant amount for a one-hour reading. More importantly, her Spiritual Master Teacher encouraged her to accept the invitation. And then she paused and a disturbing thought crossed her mind, and she said to herself…"Why do I sense that I'm being drawn into a web being spun by Emerson?" And her continuing speculation was interrupted by a caller whose impatience was wearing thin.

"OK lady, is it yes or no?"

"Well," stammered Lynn. "It's yes, but who…how…where…and when?"

"The who is a rich businessman who desires that his name not be mentioned at this time. As far as the balance of your question, there will be a chauffeured limousine to pick you up in front of your home this coming Saturday at 9:00 AM sharp. Wait at the curb and the driver will take you out east and then return you to your house safe and sound."

"Do you know my address?"

"Foolish lady, my employer knows everything that needs to be known about you and everybody else."

With that ominous statement left to linger in Lynn's ear, there was a click on the line and then silence. Stunned, Lynn held the phone in her hand unable to put it back into its cradle. Her desires were paralyzed for well over a minute. And then a child's voice entered her head saying: "It's time to bring me home."

Following her well-established routine, the evening before her reading on Long Island, Lynn quieted herself once her husband and children retired for the night. She guided herself to a spiritual place in her home where she lit a candle and bathed the room in soft soothing subdued music. Seating herself comfortably, she closed her eyes, quieted her emotions, and began a period of meditation intended to last approximately one-quarter of an hour. In no time at all, Lynn's mind transported her to an imaginary garden painted with the most brilliant depiction of flowers. Now inspired by the quietude inherent in sublime beauty, as had happened hundreds and hundreds of times before, Lynn was led to a dazzling crystal bench where she waited for her gatekeeper to usher in those with *positive* energy who were meant to join the reading the very next day.

As Lynn's mind waited patiently to receive one or more visitors, only one came. A child…a young girl several years away from reaching age ten. She sat beside Lynn with tears in her eyes and sadly said: "I miss my mommy and daddy." In a dreamlike state, Lynn saw herself embracing the child to provide comfort, and the psychic-medium felt warmth radiating throughout her body. Once tears from the child vanished so too did the child.

She reached the curb and glanced at her watch. The time that was displayed was 8:57 AM. Three minutes later, a black stretch limousine with darkened windows pulled up in front of Lynn's home. When the driver's door opened, a tall mature man introduced himself as Paul and opened the passenger door so that Lynn could take a seat. Moments later, they were *en route* to an extravagant private mansion that was deposited in the lap of ten sprawling acres in East Hampton, Long Island. The trip took a shade less than two hours traversing a six-lane highway, then a four-lane road, then a two-lane graveled pathway until they reached their destination.

The vast complex of an estate was protected from probing eyes and unwanted visitors by stone walls rising seemingly into the clouds. The twelve-foot barrier would have kept an invading army at bay had a siege taken place.

Two enormous iron gates served as the only entry point into what appeared to be a foreboding domain. The caretaker of the gateway was a husky man who sat on a bench and cradled a loaded shotgun in his arms.

Upon spotting the limo, the gatekeeper sprung to his feet and used brute force to swing open the obstruction so that the limo could easily pass. Mutual hand waves were exchanged between the driver and the security guard and then the gates were quickly closed and locked.

Two minutes later, Lynn found herself at the front door of what she would later describe to Dennis as "a palatial palace tucked into the woods." Escorted from the vehicle by the driver, Lynn was received by a man wearing a crisp black uniform and spotless white gloves who ushered her into a grand foyer the size of two spacious bedrooms.

"Madam, please follow me to the dining area. Mr. and Mrs. will visit with you shortly," came the servant's inviting words. Strange to Lynn's ears, she wondered why her hosts were not identified with names; however, she dismissed the thought expecting that the blanks would be filled in once Mr. and Mrs. made "their grand entry."

The so-called dining area was not a standard dining room. It was a banquet hall meant to entertain at least 30 guests seated and another 30 standing.

"While the gentleman and lady of the house prepare themselves to meet with you, would you care to use a bathroom to freshen up?" asked the house servant.

"No, I'm fine," remarked Lynn.

"How about a hot or cold beverage while you wait?"

"I'll have hot tea with lemon," replied the newly arrived guest.

Several minutes later, the man returned carrying a freshly polished silver tray that had a vessel filled with steaming hot water, lemon wedges neatly arranged on a decorative floral china dish, lumps of white and brown sugar in a Limoges bowl with tongs clinging to the handle, and a selection of teas from around the world.

"Would you like a tea that is sweet, nutty, fruity, floral, grassy, or slightly bitter?" asked a refined gentleman who was well-acquainted with the drink about to be served.

"Frankly, I have no preference. At home, I drink Lipton. I'm not much of a tea connoisseur. What do you recommend? I've leave the decision up to you."

"Why not try a Turkish tea. What I recommend is a particular favorite of the master of the house. It is grown in the Rize Province on the Black Sea coast."

"If it's good enough for your master, it's certainly way good enough for me," chuckled a woman who had been deposited into a fantasy world of pretentious luxury.

After preparing the tea, the affable servant excused himself explaining that he would inform his employer that "his guest was waiting to be received by him." With that, Lynn was left alone until two pairs of shoes were heard echoing as heels made contact with a marble floor signaling that one would swiftly become three.

"Welcome to our home," came a bellowing voice from a man who was at least six feet in height, slim in stature, sporting short cropped graying hair and a neatly trimmed mustache to match. He looked as though he were nearing, or had reached, 50 years in age. As his appearance grew closer, Lynn remarked to herself that he looked quite similar to the English actor named David Niven.

Short strides behind the austere gentleman trailed a woman whose demeanor boasted of seasoned breeding. Several inches shorter than her husband in height and in age, she carried herself with the stature of a model who could easily be inserted onto the next cover of *Vogue* magazine. With piercing blue eyes and flowing blond hair, she could effortlessly turn heads and slay any man's willpower.

"Let's dispense with names for the moment," as "Mr. X," as he identified himself, pulled out two chairs for himself and his wife to seat themselves across from Lynn. "Don't want to give you too much information in advance to spoil the reading."

"And you must be Mrs. X," joked Lynn as she politely took a sip of tea to conceal a smile.

"Let's get started!" exclaimed Mr. X as though he we were barking orders like a general commanding a lowly private.

"Why have you brought me so far and agreed to pay me so much?" was Lynn's need to know at the outset.

"To have you use your gift to communicate with one on the other side," replied Lynn's hostess displaying a demeanor that was direct and to the point mirroring her husband's mien.

Lynn closed her eyes as her head drifted up, as it was want to do when she began most readings.

"Why do I see a table with diamonds piled high?" questioned the psychic-medium.

"Because, that's my business," confessed Mr. X. "Mines in Central and Southern Africa and other business enterprises spread around the globe."

"Child! I am picking up the frequency of a young child. A girl. She's returned."

"Returned?" questioned the gentleman whose eyes were fixed on Lynn's.

"Yes, she visited me last night while I was meditating."

"How old?" asked Mrs. X with urgency coloring her voice as a chill rushed to greet her spine.

"Six or seven or eight. No more."

"Seven!" blurted Mrs. X unable to constrain her emotions. "Is she all right?"

Lynn paused before answering. She saw a motion picture unfolding in her mind's eye. A child being greeted by a woman of advanced age captured her attention. And then she verbalized what she had seen.

"The child was embraced upon entering Eternity's Gate by an elderly woman. Her paternal grandmother to be sure. Named? Named?

So…? Sofia? No! Sophie like the singer and comedian Sophie Tucker who just died this past February."

"Sophie was my mother's name," declared Mr. X. "Boy, you're as good as advertised. What else can you tell us about this little girl?"

"I see tainted blood on her shoes which tells me that she passed from a blood disorder or blood disease. Clearly not an accident."

"On the mark again!" shouted Mr. X with his voicing bouncing off a coffered ceiling. "Acute Monocytic Leukemia was the cruel and crippling diagnosis."

"Are we talking about your daughter or your granddaughter?"

"Lynn, a daughter. Our youngest child," confessed a mother having difficulty swallowing her distress.

"Do you have other children?" questioned Lynn.

"Two sons. One attending Harvard and one about to attend Harvard in the fall," volunteered a father with a prideful smile on his face.

"What can you tell me about our daughter? Is she in Heaven?" questioned Mrs. X.

"Heaven is a religious word that paints a picture that is often misused and misunderstood. I prefer to call the place *Beyond the Beyond*. When we leave our bodies behind, our conscious mind survives, preserving our memories, and travels to a place now hidden from the understanding of science. Our loved ones are usually met by one or more family members who have already passed on. Shortly thereafter, the newly arriving energy experiences a life review of his or her immediate past life and previous ones as well."

"Do you mean reincarnation?" asked a man with skepticism shading his beliefs.

"Yes, there is a cycle of living and dying for all of us. That cycle ends when our energy reaches a frequency that needs no further adjustment. You see, the purpose of being here in the first place is to learn life lessons. If we haven't learned all that needs to be experienced and understood, we eventually come back again and perhaps again until we do."

"Will our daughter return?" was a mother's yearning need to know.

Again Lynn hesitated before answering. She was silently asking her Spiritual Master Teacher to assist in answering the inquiry. And then a message was deposited into her spiritual vault.

"I believe that she will return one more time since her time on earth was shortened by a disease that was not of her own making."

"Will she come back to us?" was a mother's hopeful inquiry.

"Probably not. But be assured, you and your husband will reunite with your daughter when you pass through Eternity's Gate for the final time."

"Lynn, do you have insights into the meaning of life? The purpose for existence?" questioned one of the richest men in the world who thought he had all of the answers but was discovering that he didn't.

"My work has convinced me that we live in order to find and to become '*one*' with the *Source*. To achieve ultimate wisdom and love meant to last for an eternity," responded the psychic-medium. "That's the powerful message that guides me in the work that I do."

Mr. X hesitated for a moment to arrange his thoughts and to gather words.

"Let me challenge your psychic powers," declared a man who still had not revealed his name. "For this moment, while I have lost a daughter, I don't want to lose two sons. So, what can you tell me about this bloody war being fought in Southeast Asia which seems to be raging out of control?"

"My spirit guide tells me that it will last beyond the current president in office. Tens of thousands of American soldiers will die. And even more, many more, will suffer horrific wounds that will scar their minds and bodies for life. In the end, our armies will be declared losers and history will record that our government blundered badly when it sent men and women overseas to fight a senseless war."

"That's a dire prediction!" proclaimed Mr. X.

"I fear that it's not a prediction but an inevitable truth," declared the psychic-medium who had glimpsed into the future.

The reading had ended on an ominous note. True to the pre-arranged agreement, Lynn was paid handsomely for her time and then swiftly returned home as the afternoon marked the halfway point. Throughout the car ride, Lynn sat in quiet contemplation trying to grasp the meaning of the answer to the last question that she had asked Mr. and Mrs. X before leaving their home.

"I know that you are guarded about sharing your names with me, which I willing accept as protective security. But, there is one favor that I would ask. What is the name of your daughter who passed through Eternity's Gate?"

The answer that was returned in unison by two grieving parents was "Emily." And Lynn wondered to herself whether their Emily was the Emily who was visiting Milka in her dreams!

FIFTY-NINE

B radley Benjamin Barnett, completing his senior year at Columbia University, made his parents proud when the mailman delivered a letter in early April informing him that he had been accepted to the university's prestigious law school beginning in September 1966. But, his first year would be placed on hold indefinitely, with the acknowledgement of the law school's dean, so that he could fulfill a family tradition that dated back to his great-great-grandfather—military service.

Bradley was named by his father, Edward, who had served in World War II, after General of the Army Omar Nelson Bradley way before he distinguished his career further by becoming the commander of all U.S. ground forces invading Germany from the west and who later was named the first Chairman of the Joint Chiefs of Staff. Patriotism was the watchword in the Barnett household and the commemoration of Veterans Day, formerly known as Armistice Day to honor military veterans on November 11th, was treated by Edward as though it were his only religious holiday.

Bradley's great-great-grandfather, Chester, had served as a member of the 1st United States Volunteer Cavalry which saw action in 1898 during the Spanish-American War. The story passed down from one generation to the next claimed that Chester was wounded at the Battle of San Juan Hill leaving a permanent weakness on his left side which required him to walk with a cane for the balance of his life.

Chester's son, Matthew Alan, Bradley's grandfather, donned a uniform and proudly served in the 7th Infantry Division of the U.S. Army as a corporal during WWI sailing to Europe on the *SS Leviathan*. It was a standing family joke that Matthew Alan Barnett was seasick the entire voyage and couldn't wait to plant his feet on solid ground. He was remembered as saying: "I didn't mind the bullets aimed at my head as much as the waves crashing against the ship." Fortunately, Corporal Barnett was not wounded and he returned home safely once an armistice with Germany was announced on November 11, 1918 at 5:00 AM in a railroad carriage in Compiègne located in northern France.

World War I had been billed as the "War to End All Wars." So much for the misplaced optimism as Bradley's father would later attest to.

Edward William Barnett, Bradley's father, was a staff sergeant, E-6 rank, in the U.S. Army who served as a member of the 29th Infantry Division known as the "Blue and Gray." He brought home medals and horrific stories of agonizing suffering and countless men dying on the battlefield—tales of heroes displaying extraordinary courage as he and his fellow soldiers stormed Normandy Beach on D-Day, June 6, 1944. To his good fortune, Edward was not one of the 4,414 Allied casualties who never again would be embraced by a family member. Although Edward would avoid physical wounds during the war, the same could not be said for a scared psyche that would haunt him for the remainder of his life.

As Bradley was completing his final undergraduate year at Columbia, his thoughts drifted to Vietnam where his older brother, and only sibling, had been deployed as a grunt, a Marine infantryman. Kenny had joined the Marine Corp. once troop levels at home were drastically depleted and volunteers were aggressively recruited for the war effort in Southeast Asia.

Inspired by a well-established family tradition dating back almost fifty years, Bradley had signed up for Army ROTC (Reserve Officers' Training Corps) during the summer preceding the start of his senior year at Columbia. While attending college, Bradley received basic military training as well as officer training at a location nearby the university. He participated in regular drills during the school year and extended training during the summer. After graduation, in August 1966, Bradley would be sent to a military post for basic and advanced instruction, be assigned to active military duty somewhere in the world after the New Year dawned in 1967, and wear a gold-colored bar, in U.S. Army slang, a "butterbar," signifying that he was a commissioned U.S. Army officer—a second lieutenant.

When the blood drive on campus was announced, Bradley was one of the first to sign up given the fact that his brother was currently placing his life on the line fighting in Vietnam. His motivation was also paired with the growing likelihood that he would join Kenny once he graduated and completed basic military training.

The soon-to-be officer considered himself courageous, willing to die for his country. But, when it came to receiving a needle in his arm, he was, and had always been, squeamish—almost ready to faint once he saw the slender piece of metal with a sharp point advancing towards a vein.

When the day arrived for donating a pint of whole blood, March 30, 1966, Bradley did his best to think about his brother rather than his vein. Sitting in a chair in the university's gymnasium, he quickly turned away as the needle made a beeline for his arm. In no time, he had accomplished what he had set out to do to satisfy his patriotic duty.

Once the moment came to allow the next person to take his place, Bradley began to lift himself from the chair, but he immediately fell back into place. He was dizzy, and the phlebotomist on hand called for a coordinator to deliver a cup of orange juice to steady the senses of one who was no longer a donor but now a patient. And who came rushing to Bradley's side with a reviving drink? Sarah Katzman! And so began what in weeks to follow would become a full-blown romance!

Was it love at first sight? In retrospect, those asked for an opinion would echo a resounding "yes!"

A woozy Bradley, overcome by a pre-existing built-up anxiety, saw the face of what he would later describe as an "angel" once he steadied his wits and began to slowly sip from a cup of chilled nectar. Never entertaining thoughts of dating at the time, given the rigors of her studies, Sarah, unpredictably, was instantly attracted to Bradley. "Was it empathy?" some may ask. Scientists would have conjectured that it was pheromones busily at work. Had Lynn Van Praagh-Gratton been consulted, she would have pointed to another culprit—Emerson!

A seemingly "chance" meeting led to a short exchange of kind words with a promise to meet the next day in the cafeteria for lunch. A first date followed…then a second and a third… and then an introduction to their respective families…and then a commitment that advanced well-beyond friendship. A "chance" meeting at a blood drive leading to romance? Had a psychic-medium been consulted, she would have said with self-assurance: "'Chance' does not exist. Dice are not randomly tossed. There are no 'coincidences' in life!"

Sarah Katzman completed her first year at Columbia having achieved success that catapulted her onto the Dean's List. As for Bradley Barnett, he received a Bachelor of Arts diploma and headed in August across the Hudson River to Fort Dix which was located 16 miles south-southeast of Trenton, New Jersey.

Established in 1917 as Camp Dix, Fort Dix earned its name to honor Major General John Adams Dix who fought in the War of 1812 and the American Civil War. He later would become a U.S. Senator, Secretary of the Treasury, and Governor of New York State.

Bradley Barnett would receive a commission as a second lieutenant following basic and advanced military training. For the next four months, his muscles and his mind would be transported to the brink of exhaustion. Why? To prepare the junior commissioned officer to become proficient at killing and saving lives—killing an enemy and saving his life as well the members of a platoon that would number between 16 to 44 soldiers.

From the time that Bradley arrived at the training facility, until the time when he received his "marching orders," he couldn't surrender thoughts of Sarah Katzman. Although he might be able to repel an adversary's assault, it was hopeless when it came to the girl he now privately referred to as his "fiancée–to-be." He planned on popping the question once he returned from active military duty and enrolled in Columbia's law school. Until then, phone calls, love letters, a necklace consisting of two intertwining hearts, and time spent together when a weekend pass found its way into his hands would have to suffice.

For her part, Sarah had fallen head-over-heels for a second lieutenant who melted her heart, especially when he came courting in his dress uniform. She knew that she loved him and refused to glance, even innocently, at another man. But, she needed to protect her emotions. Bradley was going to war. Whether it was Vietnam, Cambodia, Laos, or some other dangerous country, she knew that he would be placed in harm's way. So, she tried to refrain from totally committing her soul as a way of coping with unthinkable possibilities.

♦

Just after the celebration of New Years 1967, Bradley was informed that he would be sent to Saigon. He would have one week to pack his gear and say his goodbyes to family, friends, and one very special young lady whose picture he carried in his wallet, on the canvas of his mind, and in the longing of his heart.

As Sarah was preparing to part with a man who her heart yearned to call her "soul mate," her passions ignited a flame of burning desire fed by her hormones and a book she had finished as part of a class assignment over the holidays.

Lady Chatterley's Lover was a controversial novel written by D. H. Lawrence in 1928 which shocked the general public by its explicit depiction of sex. The nexus of the story revolved around a young married woman named Constance Reid (Lady Chatterley) who was married to Sir Clifford Chatterley, a wealthy member of the upper crust. After suffering a paralysis from the waist down, having been wounded in the "Great War," Clifford grew depressed and the married couple's emotional and physical relationship quickly evaporated leaving Lady Chatterley to feel alone and sexually frustrated. This led her to have an affair with Oliver Mellors, the gamekeeper.

Although the novel strove to juxtapose the dominance of one socioeconomic class over another, the message was placed aside by Sarah's mind. It was the heightened sexual encounter that sent yearning chills down Sarah's spine for the first time in her young and tender life. And, it didn't take long for her mind to replace Oliver with Bradley and Lady Chatterley with herself!

Bradley spent his last evening in the States, January 23, 1967, with Sarah. It would end with more than a simple kiss on the lips!

SIXTY

F ollowing her mid-June reading with Mr. and Mrs. X, Lynn stayed loyal to her promise made to herself, her husband, and her children. She pulled down her mental curtain so as not to allow a glimmer of energy to intrude. And, as it turned out, no frequencies were shared—and that included Emerson's.

As summer and fall retreated from whence they had come, forecasters predicted a below average winter snowfall aided by milder temperatures across the northeastern sliver of the nation. As 1966 was replaced by 1967, Lynn found that her emerging celebrity stature had filled her calendar with few spaces to fill in. By February, the energy whose vibrational frequency identified itself as "Emerson" had faded from Lynn's mind like a radio signal lost during a turbulent thunderstorm. If he was true to his message and was, in fact, planning to "change his parents' lives forever" drawing her into his plans, Lynn had been denied access to his scheme for months and months. That is, until…?

Saint Valentine's Day or the Feast of Saint Valentine or simply Valentine's Day is celebrated on the 14th of February. We are told that it first appeared as a Western Christian liturgical feast to remember one or more saints named *Valentinus*.

While many myths have attached themselves to the origin of Valentine's Day, perhaps the most popular recounted the story of a priest named Valentine of Rome. Legend details that Valentine was persecuted because of his Christian faith and imprisoned by order of Roman Emperor Claudius II who visited the priest in prison intent on converting him to Roman paganism, which would have spared his life. Refusing to disown his beliefs, Valentine's fate was deprived of compassion as he was sentenced to death.

Before the date set for his execution, the priest is said to have performed a miracle, healing the blind daughter of his jailer, Asterius, whose
child's name was Julia. Writing a letter to the young girl before his punishment was carried out, Valentine signed the writing with the salutation
"Your Valentine." Thereafter, Valentine was canonized as a saint and the
holiday eventually took on meaning as a day to honor love, especially
deeply-cherished romantic love.

Tuesday, February 14, 1967, started out with a light afternoon dust-
ing of snow which left only the slimmest coating when evening arrived.
While Lynn waited patiently at home for her husband, Dennis abbreviated
his work day an hour earlier in order to pick up a dozen long-stemmed red
roses and a gourmet box of Belgium hand-dipped chocolates. With the
children now fully capable of caring for themselves, it was possible for two
soul mates to steal away for a candlelit romantic evening at their favorite
Italian restaurant where a table in a corner had been reserved, days in
advance, to allow for intimacy.

Once the door was opened and kisses were shared not once but
twice, the roses were escorted to a finely crafted crystal vase while the
chocolates found a hiding place beyond the reach of a child's probing
hand.

The evening lived up to its designed intentions as Lynn and Dennis
toasted to their love and exchanged soulful emotions. But, like all special
moments in life, as quickly as the moment was realized, it employed the
same haste to leave, only to be preserved as a fleeting memory.

With the car safely parked in the garage, Lynn realized that no one
had picked up the mail that had been delivered that day. So, she left Dennis
for a minute to reach into the box. To her surprise, there was only one piece
of mail, a small package addressed to her that had no sender's name and
return address, no stamps, and no post office impression to show that the
U.S. government had had a *hand* in delivering it. "How strange," she confided to herself. "How very strange indeed!"

Waiting to open the package until she got settled in the house, Lynn
placed it on an entry table while she removed her coat and gloves. Forget-

ting about it for an instant, she checked on her children who were all fast asleep and then she retired to her bedroom to change her clothes and don nightwear. By this time, Dennis had already prepared himself for bed and was laying with the back of his head snuggly sunken into his pillow. A healthy yawn suggested that he was seconds away from closing his eyes for the next seven hours.

Remembering that the package had been abandoned in the vestibule, Lynn went to retrieve it. Once she opened it and pulled out the contents, she discovered that someone had sent her a book that contained a compendium of essays and poems penned by Ralph Waldo Emerson. "How strange," she muttered until she repeated the name "Emerson" aloud, and an inner voice whispered: "The boy not the poet!"

As Lynn quickly thumbed through the volume guided by a need to satisfy the wishes of another, her right hand suddenly stopped when she found a dime inserted at the start of an essay entitled *The Over-Soul*. "How very peculiar," she cautioned herself recognizing that the coin represented the presence of an energy engaging her attention from *Beyond the Beyond*. And the subject matter of this particular composition?

Still steps away from her bedroom door, Lynn noticed that an editor had inserted comments preceding Emerson's essay. The editorial annotation informed the reader:

Published in 1841, there are four general themes:

(1)   The existence and nature of the human soul;
(2)   The relationship between the soul and the personal ego;
(3)   The relationship of one human soul to another;
(4)   The relationship of the human soul to God.

No addressor…no postage stamps to ensure delivery…no processing stamp to identify the handling…a work by a distinguished poet who happened to be named Emerson…a dime stuck in the binding on a page that spoke to metaphysics. For Lynn, there was only one conclusion to be drawn—Emerson had finally returned after *months and months* of a silent absence! And then she reminded herself: "There is no such thing as *time* to those residing *Beyond the Beyond*."

Why she decided to close the book and secret it with the dime inserted in the book's spine under her pillow before retiring for bed, she wouldn't be able to explain, except that she intuitively sensed that it needed to be done. And, when she awoke in the morning, her deliberate action had acquired validation.

When Lynn's eyes caught the first glimmer of the morning sun following Valentine's Day, she found that Dennis had quietly removed himself from bed so as not to disturb his soundly sleeping wife. Wondering why her pillow seemed so firm, she suddenly recalled the collection of essays and poems of Ralph Waldo Emerson tucked under her head while she had slept. "What a ridiculous thing to do!" she thought to herself until the voice of a young man counseled otherwise.

Sitting up in bed, Lynn tilted her head as she closed her eyes tightly. Now immersing herself in meditative contemplation, a movie began to play in her mind. It was reliving a dream that had visited her overnight, a reverie built upon a foundation of prophesy.

The drama unfolded on March 17, 1967, only a month and two days away. How did Lynn know with certitude the month…day…and year? Because she saw herself holding a newspaper in her hand with that specific date emblazoned across the top of the front page. Where was she heading after briskly leaving home at 10:00 AM? To New York City's Central Park. Why? To sit beside a young girl wearing a white faux fur winter coat, white mittens, and a white knit beanie to insulate herself from the cold. What was the young lady doing? Sobbing unendingly. Because? She had lost a loved one. And? She was harboring a deeply-held secret kept from family and friends. And then? Lynn asked to sit beside her to console her. Were the two alone on the bench? No! Two vibrational energies had joined them with their frequencies felt only by the psychic-medium. And then the last clip on the movie's reel abruptly ended without revealing an outcome. Why?

Lynn took a healthy breath for she suddenly sensed a presence in the bedroom. Opening her eyes and then turning her head towards the entry door, she spied the silhouette of a young man approaching intent on conveying a message. And, as rapidly as the shadow appeared, it just as quickly vanished leaving these lingering words to burrow deep inside Lynn's brain: "Destiny will be waiting to greet you on the 17th of March, on a bench in Central Park, with a young girl unknowingly awaiting your arrival!"

SIXTY-ONE

F antasy or reality? Prophetic or foolish? The dream that Lynn had had four weeks earlier spoke of the future, in her mind, a future colored by certainty! The gift that had shadowed her throughout her life, speaking to those dwelling *Beyond the Beyond*, was preparing to weave her into the tapestry of tomorrow—tomorrow being March 17, 1967 on a bench in Central Park. Would she choose to go on that day or fight with all her will to resist? The choice was not hers to make and she knew it. Why? Because her intentions were guided by the *hand* of another.

On the evening of March 16th, Lynn prepared herself as though the next day was meant to be a formal reading. She guided herself to a spiritual place in her home where she had lit a candle countless times before and then turned on a radio to a pre-set station to bathe the room in soft soothing background music. Seating herself comfortably, she tightly shut her eyes, quieted her emotions, and began a period of meditation. In no time, Lynn's mind escorted her to an imaginary garden painted with the most colorful flowers of varying shades. Now inspired by the tranquility intrinsic in tran- scendent beauty, as had happened numerous times before, Lynn was led to an alluring crystal bench where she waited for her gatekeeper to usher in those with **positive** vibrating energy.

The only specter of a person who chose to sit beside her was a young man dressed in a green uniform with an erratic frequency that had difficulty modulating its/his intensity. This suggested to Lynn that the energy had just recently passed through Eternity's Gate. When words formed in Lynn's mind, she could barely make out a subdued softness that was tinged with melancholy regrets.

"There was so much more for me to do," he bemoaned, as the psy- chic-medium absorbed and processed his message in her mind. "Why am I here?" A satisfying answer did not deposit itself into Lynn's channeled ear. "Unfinished business! Unfinished business!" the voice from *Beyond the Beyond* persisted.

When Lynn telepathically asked: "What business?" No reply was received. Fighting to continue to meld with the man's vibrational frequency, Lynn dispensed with hope. The connection had been lost; but she was certain that tomorrow in the park would produce a different outcome.

She sat alone on a wooden bench in New York City's Central Park on March 17th bundled up to insulate her body's internal heat from an outdoor temperature that dipped below 32 degrees Fahrenheit. To those passing by, she looked like a giant snow bunny dressed in a white faux fur winter coat, wearing white mittens and a white knit beanie. She was holding a letter laced with regrets as tears flooded her face. It was a copy of a military notice with the original having been placed in the hands of two grieving parents. Bradley Benjamin Barnett had been KIA ("Killed In Action") while serving his country were the words printed in boldface type.

Bradley and several members of his platoon had been in a café in Saigon spending one last night in the capital city of South Vietnam before being sent to the Mekong Delta west of the city. It was meant to be a respite before embarking upon an expedition that would have brought the infantrymen face-to-face with an elusive and dangerous enemy. Little did anyone know that a North Vietnamese sympathizer had planted a bomb with a detonator timed for 7:30 PM when the premises would be entertaining military personnel and civilians. In total, twenty-three people were killed and scores were wounded. Amongst the dead was Second Lieutenant Bradley Barnett who, when found, was buried in a pile of debris of metal, glass, and wood framing.

As Sarah Katzman read the official Army death notice over and over and over again, she fought to accept the truth that Bradley was gone "forever." There was something that she needed desperately to tell him but now the message could never be conveyed. Or could it?

Lynn readied herself for a visit to Central Park once she rose earlier than the beeping of her alarm clock. She had told Dennis that she was scheduled for a very early morning reading but kept the truth to herself not wanting to unduly frighten him. "Emerson is up to something," Lynn confided to herself as she applied her makeup, and then she remembered his punctuated message:

"I am preparing to change my parents' lives forever
and I need your help to assist me with my plan!"

Recalling the dream that took command of her day, Lynn left her home at 10:00 AM destined to arrive at New York's famed park at an hour appointed and anointed by fate. Having dressed warmly to keep out the chill, she waited for a reserved taxi to take her to her destination; and, the driver pulled up right on time. Although the park was large and it might prove difficult to find the girl in question, Lynn had no concerns because she knew that her Spiritual Master Teacher would direct her feet down the proper pathway. And her intuitive instincts squarely hit the mark.

It took Lynn no more than five minutes, once she exited the cab, to find the young lady in languishing distress. Approaching her with deliberate caution, Lynn introduced herself and asked if she could take a seat beside her. Although Sarah wanted to maintain her privacy, somehow she couldn't deny the request of a stranger who had a face that communicated unpretentious kindness.

"What's your name?" asked Lynn in a tonal whisper.
"Sarah. Sarah Katzman."
"And mine is lengthy to write," laughed the psychic-medium trying to erase any tension. "It's Lynn Van Praagh-Gratton. But please, simply call me Lynn."
"And you can call me Sarah."
"Well Sarah, providence has arranged for us to meet. You see, I'm a psychic-medium. I won't trouble you with the details that inspired me to come to Central Park this morning. Just know that while meditating last night, a gentleman wearing a green uniform visited my conscious awareness. He's a young man who recently passed through Eternity's Gate to no longer reside with we here on Earth. Am I making any sense?"
"Truly," whimpered Sarah as she wiped tears from her eyes as some drops froze to her cheek. "He's my boyfriend who was destined to

become a lifelong soul mate. His name is, or was, Bradley. He was an Army officer. He was killed in Vietnam."

Lynn hesitated. As had been foretold in her dream, two frequencies suddenly entered into the psychic-medium's "circle of hearing and understanding."

"Sarah, the energy possessed by the young soldier you call 'Bradley' just sat down beside you. And now, next to me, is one known to me as 'Emerson.'"

Sarah instinctively turned her torso to the right, but she saw nothing. Moving her hands with a sweeping motion, she felt nothing. Speaking words of love to her lover, she heard no reply.

"Is Bradley speaking? What does he say? Lynn, does he have a message for me?"

"Sarah, he says that he loves you now and always, and that when you pass through Eternity's Gate he'll be waiting for you and for another."

"Another?"

"Sarah, he says that he knows your secret and is elated. Yes, he's using the word 'elated' to describe his understanding of what he calls 'the truth.' And there's more."

"More?" responded Sarah with excitement replacing sorrow.

"Yes, he sees a little girl asleep in your belly. He knows her name but will allow you to discover it later on."

"He knows that I'm pregnant with his child, a girl, and that I haven't told my parents or his?"

"He knows this and other things."

"Like what Lynn? Like what?"

"That the child will be raised by a loving couple so that you can complete your studies. He says that at your tender age, you can't devote enough time to the baby's care while, at the same time, trying to move along with your life to fulfill the reason why you are here on earth."

"The reason why I am here on earth?" repeated Sarah anxious to know the hidden implication.

"To become a role model for women around the world!" was the message conveyed by Bradley to Lynn to repeat to Sarah.

"How? A role model for women?" questioned Sarah.

"Sarah, he said that it is not for him to tell. Rather, it is for you to experience with joy as one Earth-year passes to another."

"What about the baby?" questioned Sarah aloud hoping to connect to Bradley's energy.

"That's why another vibrating energy has joined me," replied Bradley through Lynn's lips, clearly referencing Emerson.

"Yes Bradley. Why? Tell me why?" pleaded Sarah as she shifted her eyes in order to look directly into Lynn's eyes.

"There is a couple who lost a son," began the psychic-medium fetching words from Bradley carried with him from *Beyond the Beyond*. "The son is here with me now. His earthly name was Emerson. His frequency has connected with mine to finish his story, an unfinished story lacking a happy ending for his parents. Strangely, you know Emerson's mother and your father knows Emerson's father."

"Mother? Father?" reiterated Sarah with a question mark glued to each word.

"The mother, Emerson tells me, is a woman who worked with you at the blood drive when we first met."

"Milka? Is her name Milka?"

"Yes, Sarah," came Bradley's confirmation.

"I know her well and value her continuing friendship," was Sarah's reply displaying a confused smile.

"The father, Emerson also says, is named Josip. It seems that Josip met your father when your dad shopped at Josip's clothing store."

"What a coincidence!" exclaimed Sarah until Lynn's pointer finger gently touched her cheek and the medium whispered: "There are no coincidences in life."

"Sarah, the energy called 'Emerson' was one of the first to welcome me when I passed through Eternity's Gate. He is wise, and his wisdom is drawn from many lifetime incarnations and from what here is called the *Source*."

"What wisdom does he offer?" Sarah asked Lynn to ask Bradley.

"The woman who I speak through is blessed with charity of the heart. I and destiny now call upon her to arrange a meeting of three families—yours, mine, and Emerson's. Once gathered together as one, you must tell them the glorious news of our daughter's planned arrival. Express a desire, our desire, that Milka and Josip take the baby into their care freeing your family and my family of the burden and, at the same time, bringing infinite joy to Emerson's parents who lost their **only** child. Know that I have seen well into the future, a future that has no beginning and no ending; and, the *Source* has told me that our daughter will aspire to greatness just like her biological mother and, eventually, you, I, and she will become '*one with eternity.*'"

Bradley's frequency was waning, exhausted and growing faint like the energy of a fire deprived of oxygen.

"Sarah, Bradley and Emerson are gone," were Lynn's words as she took a deep breath to relax her drained emotions. "That leaves just you and me and the reason I was drawn to you today in the first place."

"Reason?" queried Sarah.

"To find a loving and caring home for your daughter so that, in Bradley's word, you can realize your destiny…'to become a role model for women around the world!'"

EPILOGUE

S he arrived on October 23, 1967 welcomed into the world by a mother and three sets of families. Sarah cradled her precious bundled of joy in her arms during her three-day stay in the hospital, frequently remarking that the baby possessed Bradley's eyes and his ebullient smile. A bond between Sarah and her daughter had been forged the moment that the newborn had entered man's earthly plane of existence, a union designed by the *Source* to continue until the two joined the ***light and love*** of eternity's embrace.

When asked for the name on the birth certificate, Sarah paused to remind herself of her favorite poetess, a reclusive woman who, next to Walt Whitman, has been lauded as the most important American poet of the nineteenth century, having produced in one lifetime over 1,800 works.

"My daughter will be called 'Emily Elizabeth,'" declared Sarah, the literature major, "after the famous poet Emily Elizabeth Dickinson."

Sarah would not become a stranger to the Weiss household once custody of Emily was entrusted to parents who had raised a brilliant son. No, to the contrary! Milka and Josip, as days blended into weeks, and then months, and eventually years, welcomed Sarah into their lives like a daughter. As Milka would come to affectionately call her..."Our daughter-mother." And Emily? She had been a blessing gift-wrapped by one who had made this promise to Lynn Van Praagh-Gratton from *Beyond the Beyond*:

> ***"I am preparing to change my parents' lives forever***
> ***and I need your help to assist me with my plan!"***

◆

Lynn relished, with prideful satisfaction, her work as a psychic-medium because it brought healing, solace, acceptance, hope, joy, knowledge, and wisdom to those struggling to deal with the grief borne by the loss of a loved one. Her continuing message mirrored the one that Emerson had left in the hearts of his parents before departing for Eternity's Gate:

"The day which we fear as our last is but the birthday of eternity."

When hearing of the birth of Emily Elizabeth, Lynn smiled as she recalled Milka's reoccurring dreams about a little girl named Emily who knocked on Milka's door looking for a permanent home. And then Lynn's smile increased as she remembered that Mr. and Mrs. X had lost a daughter named Emily who was meant to return to Earth to complete an unfinished life. Two disjointed coincidences? "There are no coincidences in life!" the psychic-medium reminded herself.

During Lynn's first reading with Milka and Josip Weiss, she had channeled these words communicated by their son:

> "There is what I can best describe as a 'spiritual mountain' here, not seen but felt, which is constructed of layers of frequencies or vibrations. Once we leave Earth for good, we must try to scale to the summit to reach the highest frequency where the *Source* resides. Why? To experience the perfection of light, love, and understanding.
>
> "How can I and others ascend upwards towards the pinnacle to achieve eternal fulfillment? It seems by inspiring those back on Earth to bring their lives in harmony with the *Source's* universal frequency. By offering guidance in ways that I'm just learning about. If those entrusted to my care make progress back on Earth, so too, I will make progress here rising to the top of the 'spiritual mountain.'

"Look for signs that I am around you. I will be guiding you. Inspiring you. By helping you, I am, at the same time, helping myself to be one with the *Source* and to achieve ultimate wisdom, which was my driving need when I lived as Emerson."

Emily Elizabeth brought Milka and Josip's lives "into harmony with the *Source's* universal frequency" guided by a *hand* that reached from *Beyond the Beyond*. And Emerson's reward? He rose to the summit of a spiritual mountain, becoming *one* with the eternal cosmos where he experienced the perfection of light, love, and understanding!

BIOGRAPHICAL FOOTNOTES

Lynn Van Praagh-Gratton...

The biographical information included in chapter Fifty-Two of this book is a true and accurate depiction of my life story with this exception—dates have been adjusted or eliminated in order to compliment the story being told. For the reader, I would like to amplify my personal biography by providing these few additional details.

Dennis and I were privileged to have four wonderful children together and they have blessed us with seven amazing grandchildren. Family has brought, and continues to bring, joyous celebration to my life; and, each day that I am privileged to live, I express gratitude expressed from my heart intended to last beyond eternity.

What inspires my life's work has been, and always will be, spreading "**Love**, **Light**, and **Understanding**" to as many people as possible until my voice grows silent. The message that I convey to those stricken by despairing grief is that there is, in fact, "**life after death**."

As time advances, I find myself constantly in the air or on the road traveling throughout our great country to share my healing *gift* of being able to communicate with those who have passed through *Eternity's Gate* to reside *Beyond the Beyond*. What gives me strength and inspiration, with each new day, is the knowledge that I was given the unique opportunity to wipe away another's tears and soothe another's aching heart!

For those who may wish to contact me, kindly be advised of the following:

Lynnvanpraagh-Gratton.com (e-mail address)
Lynnvanpraagh-Gratton (Facebook page)
917-882-1391 (phone number)

Brett Stephan Bass...

With the same ambitious drive as Emerson Alexander Weiss in the two-part story of his life and afterlife, **Brett Stephan Bass** has dedicated the past 20 years (of his 70 years) trying to make sense of the confusing conundrum interwoven into the fabric of human existence—the meaning of life! How? By burying his head in well over 100 books that addressed: modern-day understanding of science— especially astronomy, cosmology, paleoanthropology (human evolution), and quantum mechanics; by immersing himself in the history and expansion of Western and Eastern religions; and, by contemplating the musings of past and contemporary philosophers. And also? By traveling with his best friend and soul mate, his wife, Rosalind Charlotte, to every continent and over 70 countries to strive to decode the beliefs and intuitive instincts and teachings of others.

Brett Stephan Bass has fashioned his life's mission buttressed by four foundational footings: (1) The perfection of "**_LOVE_**," more particularly, his adoration for his wife; (2) The consumption of a thirst-quenching elixir called "**_KNOWLEDGE_**"; (3) The inspiration offered by "**_EXPERIENCE_**" which challenges _Homo sapiens_ to give the phrase, "to be alive," a defining meaning and purpose; and (4) The need to dispense with a course charted by traditional science, religion, and philosophy in order to follow a compass that points one in the direction of "**_SPIRITUALITY_**."

Brett's career path led him first to the law where his talents were harnessed as a litigator and as an appellate attorney. Then, he transitioned and became a business entrepreneur. Now retired, seven years ago he unexpectedly was blessed with the gift of auto-writing novels—story after story arrived mysteriously in his brain seemingly out of thin air. With this latest work, he has added twelve narratives to the bookshelves of others.